# EDWARD ALBEE

## THE PLAYS

# EDWARD ALBEE

## VOLUME ONE

*The Zoo Story*
*The Death of Bessie Smith*
*The Sandbox*
*The American Dream*

# THE PLAYS

*Coward, McCann & Geoghegan*

NEW YORK

Library of Congress Cataloging in Publication Data

Albee, Edward, date.
    Selected plays.

        Vol. 2–4 published by Atheneum Press.
        Contents: v. 1. The zoo story. The death of Bessie
    Smith. The sandbox. The American dream — v. 2. Tiny
    Alice. A delicate balance. Box and Quotations from
    Chairman. Mao Tse-Tung — [etc.]
        I. Title.
    PS3551.L25A19      1981        812'.54        81-3613
                                                  AACR2
    ISBN 0-698-11092-7 (pbk.:v. 1)

Printed in the United States of America

# Contents

# *Introduction*

One evening, twenty-three years ago, I "borrowed" a hundred sheets or so of poor quality yellow typing paper from the Western Union office where I was employed as a messenger boy, brought it back to my Greenwich Village walk-up and placed it on the rickety kitchen table next to my battered non-portable typewriter. Three weeks later, fifty some sheets of the yellow paper had become a play, and I had become a playwright.

Everyone was surprised, and no one more than I. I had known I was *something*—poet, novelist, short story writer, *something*— but I had not dreamed of playwriting until all of a sudden I did it. Thereafter, of course, inevitability set in and the endless ride began.

Shortly after *The Zoo Story* was completed, and while it was being read and politely refused by a number of New York producers (which was not unexpected, for no one at all had ever heard of its author, and it *was* a short play, and short plays *are*, unfortunately, anathema to producers and—supposedly—to audiences), a young composer friend of mine, William Flanagan by name, looked at the play, liked it, and sent it to several friends of his, among them David Diamond, another American composer, resident in Italy; Diamond liked the play and sent it on to a friend of *his*, a Swiss actor, Pinkas Braun; Braun liked the play, made a tape recording of it, playing both its roles, which he sent to Mrs. Stefani Hunzinger, who headed the drama department of the S. Fischer Verlag, a large publishing house in Frankfurt; she, in turn . . . well, through her it got to Berlin, and to production. From New York to Florence to Zurich to Frankfurt to Berlin. And finally back to New York where, on January 14, 1960, it received American production, off Broadway, at the Province-town Playhouse, on a double bill with Samuel Beckett's *Krapp's Last Tape*.

I went to Berlin for the opening of *The Zoo Story.* I had not planned to—it seemed like such a distance, such an expense— but enough friends said to me that, of course, I would be present at the first performance of my first play that I found myself, quickly enough, replying, yes, yes, of course; I wouldn't miss it for the world. And so, I went; and I *wouldn't* have missed it for the world. I wouldn't have missed it for the world, despite the fact—as I have learned since—that, for this author, at least, opening nights do not really exist. They happen, but they take place as if in a dream: One concentrates, but one cannot see the stage action clearly; one can hear but barely; one tries to follow the play, but one can make no sense of it. And, if one is called to the stage afterward to take a bow, one wonders why, for one can make no connection between the work just presented and one's self. Naturally, this feeling was complicated in the case of *The Zoo Story*, as the play was being presented in German, a language of which I knew not a word, and in Berlin, too, an awesome city. But, it has held true since. The high points of a person's life can be appreciated so often only in retrospect.

The Death of Bessie Smith also had its premiere in Berlin, while *The Sandbox* was done first in New York.

The Death of Bessie Smith began in my mind as a statement of (somewhat tardy) outrage over the racial prejudice in the South in the '30s which resulted in the singer's death, and emerged on the page as that, but became, as well, a socio-economic examination of a time and place. I had not been to the South when I wrote the play, and I was barely conscious during the period of its setting, but Southerners old enough to remember tell me it's all on target.

The Sandbox, which is fourteen minutes long, was written to satisfy a commission from the Festival of Two Worlds for a short dramatic piece for the Festival's summer program in Spoleto, Italy—where it was not performed. I was, at the time of the commission, at work on a rather longer play, *The American Dream.* For *The Sandbox*, I extracted several of the characters from *The American Dream* and placed them in a situation different from, but related to, their predicament in the longer play. They seemed happy out of doors, in *The Sandbox*, nor were they distressed to be back in a stuffy apartment, in *The American Dream.*

All four of these plays received generally favorable and now and again intelligent and useful reviews when they were first performed—both in Europe and the United States. (Indeed, *The Zoo Story* ran for three years off Broadway, and all of them have entrenched themselves in the colleges, the adventuresome regional theaters and the other crannies where serious short work hangs for its life.) *The American Dream* received its share of favorable press, but I would like to concern myself here with some of the bad—not because I am a masochist, but because I would like to point up, foolhardy though it may be of me, what I consider to be a misuse of the critical function in American press letters.

For example: The off-Broadway critic for one of New York's morning tabloids had his sensibilities (or something) so offended by the *content* of *The American Dream* that he refused to review the next play of mine that opened.

Another example: A couple of other critics (bright gentlemen who do their opinions for intellectualist weekly sheets of—sadly, all in all—very small circulation) went all to pieces over the (to their mind) nihilist, immoral, defeatist *content* of the play. And so on.

May I submit that when a critic sets himself up as an arbiter of morality, a judge of the matter and not the manner of a work, he is no longer a critic but a censor.

And just what is the *content* of *The American Dream* (a comedy, yet) that so upset these guardians of the public morality? The play is an examination of the American Scene, an attack on the substitution of artificial for real values in our society, a condemnation of complacency, cruelty, emasculation and vacuity; it is a stand against the fiction that everything in this slipping land of ours is peachy-keen.

Is the play offensive? I certainly hope so; it was my intention to offend—as well as to amuse and to entertain. Is it nihilist, immoral, defeatist? Well, to that let me answer that *The American Dream* is a picture of our time—as I see it, of course. Every honest work is a personal, private yowl, a statement of one individual's pleasure or pain, but I hope that *The American Dream* is something more than that. I hope that it transcends the personal and the private, and has something to do with the anguish of us all.

Now—1981—I am nineteen plays into what I believe is referred to as my "career" and am, at least to my sense of it, about halfway along the road. Thirty-eight or forty plays would be a nice number to end up with, and I intend to keep writing toward that goal so long as my ideas hold out.

I wonder what I have learned along the way? Not much, probably, but something. I have learned, for example, that experimental plays, dense, unfamiliar and lacking proper road signs, meet with considerable critical and audience hostility, but that when I feel the fit that results in one of these coming on, there is nothing for it but to wince, write it, take the caning, and hope that the next one will be "easier" for everybody. I have learned that some of my subjects—how we lie to ourselves and to each other, how we try to live without the cleansing consciousness of death, for example—are not the stuff of box office smash, and sometimes, not very often, but sometimes, I wish I could write about what Herbert Gold called "happy problems." I have learned that while I am especially fond of those plays of mine that have been most misunderstood, I must not misunderstand the feeling, that this fondness is not necessarily a valid intellectual judgement and may, indeed, be nothing more than protective parenthood: touching, but not always instructive. I have learned that being a playwright (like being a politician, or an ax murderer) is what one *is* more than merely what one does, and that a playwright's perceptions are framed by the proscenium arch. The truth he tells is a playwright's truth but, with any luck "it transcends the personal and the private, and has something to do with the anguish of us all."

Edward Albee
New York City
1960; 1961; 1981

# *The Zoo Story*

A PLAY IN ONE SCENE (1958)

*For William Flanagan*

FIRST PERFORMANCE
September 28, 1959, Berlin, Germany.

Schiller Theater Werkstatt.


FIRST AMERICAN PERFORMANCE
January 14, 1960, New York City.

The Provincetown Playhouse.

# THE PLAYERS:

### PETER

A man in his early forties, neither fat nor gaunt, neither handsome nor homely. He wears tweeds, smokes a pipe, carries horn-rimmed glasses. Although he is moving into middle age, his dress and his manner would suggest a man younger.

### JERRY

A man in his late thirties, not poorly dressed, but carelessly. What was once a trim and lightly muscled body has begun to go to fat; and while he is no longer handsome, it is evident that he once was. His fall from physical grace should not suggest debauchery; he has, to come closest to it, a great weariness.

# THE SCENE

It is Central Park; a Sunday afternoon in summer; the present. There are two park benches, one toward either side of the stage; they both face the audience. Behind them: foliage, trees, sky. At the beginning, Peter is seated on one of the benches.

*(As the curtain rises,* PETER *is seated on the bench stage-right. He is reading a book. He stops reading, cleans his glasses, goes back to reading.* JERRY *enters.)*

### JERRY

I've been to the zoo. (PETER *doesn't notice*) I said, I've been to the zoo. MISTER, I'VE BEEN TO THE ZOO!

### PETER

Hm? . . . What? . . . I'm sorry, were you talking to me?

### JERRY

I went to the zoo, and then I walked until I came here. Have I been walking north?

### PETER *(Puzzled)*

North? Why . . . I . . . I think so. Let me see.

### JERRY

*(Pointing past the audience)* Is that Fifth Avenue?

### PETER

Why yes; yes, it is.

### JERRY

And what is that cross street there; that one, to the right?

PETER

That? Oh, that's Seventy-fourth Street.

JERRY

And the zoo is around Sixty-fifth Street; so, I've been walking north.

PETER

(*Anxious to get back to his reading*) Yes; it would seem so.

JERRY

Good old north.

PETER

(*Lightly, by reflex*) Ha, ha.

JERRY

(*After a slight pause*) But not due north.

PETER

I . . . well, no, not due north; but, we . . . call it north. It's northerly.

JERRY

(*Watches as* PETER, *anxious to dismiss him, prepares his pipe*) Well, boy; you're not going to get lung cancer, are you?

PETER

(*Looks up, a little annoyed, then smiles*) No, sir. Not from this.

JERRY

No, sir. What you'll probably get is cancer of the mouth, and then you'll have to wear one of those things Freud wore after they took one whole side of his jaw away. What do they call those things?

PETER *(Uncomfortable)*

A prosthesis?

JERRY

The very thing! A prosthesis. You're an educated man, aren't you? Are you a doctor?

PETER

Oh, no; no. I read about it somewhere; *Time* magazine, I think. *(He turns to his book)*

JERRY

Well, *Time* magazine isn't for blockheads.

PETER

No, I suppose not.

JERRY

*(After a pause)* Boy, I'm glad that's Fifth Avenue there.

PETER *(Vaguely)*

Yes.

JERRY

I don't like the west side of the park much.

PETER

Oh? *(Then, slightly wary, but interested)* Why?

JERRY *(Offhand)*

I don't know.

PETER

Oh. *(He returns to his book)*

JERRY

*(He stands for a few seconds, looking at* PETER, *who finally looks up again, puzzled)* Do you mind if we talk?

PETER

*(Obviously minding)* Why . . . no, no.

JERRY

Yes you do; you do.

PETER

*(Puts his book down, his pipe out and away, smiling)* No, really; I don't mind.

JERRY

Yes you do.

PETER

*(Finally decided)* No; I don't mind at all, really.

JERRY

It's . . . it's a nice day.

PETER
*(Stares unnecessarily at the sky)* Yes. Yes, it is; lovely.


JERRY
I've been to the zoo.


PETER
Yes, I think you said so . . . didn't you?


JERRY
Probably. Who listens if you say something only once? *You* have TV, don't you?


PETER
Why yes, we have two; one for the children.


JERRY
You're married!


PETER
*(With pleased emphasis)* Why, certainly.


JERRY
It isn't a law, for God's sake.


PETER
No . . . no, of course not.


JERRY
And you have a wife.

PETER

*(Bewildered by the seeming lack of communication)* Yes!

JERRY

And you have children.

PETER

Yes; two.

JERRY

Boys?

PETER

No, girls . . . both girls.

JERRY

But you wanted boys.

PETER

Well . . . naturally, every man wants a son, but . . .

JERRY

*(Lightly mocking)* But that's the way the cookie crumbles?

PETER *(Annoyed)*

I wasn't going to say that.

JERRY

And you're not going to have any more kids, are you?

PETER

*(A bit distantly)* No. No more. *(Then back, and irksome)*
Why did you say that? How would you know about that?

JERRY
The way you cross your legs, perhaps; something in the voice.
Or maybe I'm just guessing. Is it your wife?

PETER *(Furious)*
That's none of your business! *(A silence)* Do you understand?
*(JERRY nods. PETER is quiet now)* Well, you're right. We'll
have no more children.

JERRY *(Softly)*
That *is* the way the cookie crumbles.

PETER *(Forgiving)*
Yes . . . I guess so.

JERRY
Well, now; what else?

PETER
What were you saying about the zoo . . . ?

JERRY
I'll tell you about it, soon. Do you mind if I ask you
questions?

PETER
Oh, not really.

JERRY
I'll tell you why I do it; I don't talk to many people—except to
say like: give me a beer, or where's the john, or what time
does the feature go on, or keep your hands to yourself, buddy.
You know—things like that.

PETER

I must say I don't . . .

JERRY

But every once in a while I like to talk to somebody, really *talk*; like to get to know somebody, know all about him.

PETER

*(Lightly laughing, still a little uncomfortable)* And am I the guinea pig for today?

JERRY

On a sun-drenched Sunday afternoon like this? Who better than a nice married man with two daughters and . . . uh . . . a dog? (PETER *shakes his head*) No? Two dogs. (PETER *shakes his head again*) Hm. No dogs? (PETER *shakes his head, sadly*) Oh, that's a shame. But you look like an animal man. CATS? (PETER *nods his head, ruefully*) Cats! But, that can't be your idea. No, sir. Your wife and daughters? (PETER *nods his head*) Is there anything else I should know?

PETER

*(He has to clear his throat)* There are . . . there are two parakeets. One . . . uh . . . one for each of my daughters.

JERRY

Birds.

PETER

My daughters keep them in a cage in their bedroom.

JERRY

Do they carry disease? The birds.

PETER

I don't believe so.


JERRY

That's too bad. If they did you could set them loose in the
house and the cats could eat them and die, maybe. (PETER
*looks blank for a moment, then laughs*) And what else? What
do you do to support your enormous household?


PETER

I . . . uh . . . I have an executive position with a . . . a small
publishing house. We . . . uh . . . we publish textbooks.


JERRY

That sounds nice; very nice. What do you make?


PETER *(Still cheerful)*

Now look here!


JERRY

Oh, come on.


PETER

Well, I make around thirty-eight thousand a year, but I don't
carry more than forty dollars at any one time . . . in case
you're a . . . a holdup man . . . ha, ha, ha.


JERRY

*(Ignoring the above)* Where do you live? (PETER *is reluctant*)
Oh, look; I'm not going to rob you, and I'm not going to
kidnap your parakeets, your cats, or your daughters.

PETER *(Too loud)*
I live between Lexington and Third Avenue, on Seventy-fourth Street.

JERRY
That wasn't so hard, was it?

PETER
I didn't mean to seem . . . ah . . . it's that you don't really carry on a conversation; you just ask questions. And I'm . . . I'm normally . . . uh . . . reticent. Why do you just stand there?

JERRY
I'll start walking around in a little while, and eventually I'll sit down. *(Recalling)* Wait until you see the expression on his face.

PETER
What? Whose face? Look here; is this something about the zoo?

JERRY *(Distantly)*
The what?

PETER
The zoo; the zoo. Something about the zoo.

JERRY
The zoo?

PETER
You've mentioned it several times.

JERRY

*(Still distant, but returning abruptly)* The zoo? Oh, yes; the zoo. I was there before I came here. I told you that. Say, what's the dividing line between upper-middle-middle-class and lower-upper-middle-class?

PETER

My dear fellow, I . . .

JERRY

Don't my dear fellow me.

PETER *(Unhappily)*

Was I patronizing? I believe I was; I'm sorry. But, you see your question about the classes bewildered me.

JERRY

And when you're bewildered you become patronizing?

PETER

I . . . I don't express myself too well, sometimes. *(He attempts a joke on himself)* I'm in publishing, not writing.

JERRY

*(Amused, but not at the humor)* So be it. The truth *is: I* was being patronizing.

PETER

Oh, now; you needn't say that.
> *(It is at this point that Jerry may begin to move about the stage with slowly increasing determination and authority, but pacing himself, so that the long speech about the dog comes at the high point of the arc)*

JERRY

All right. Who are your favorite writers? Baudelaire and James
Michener?

PETER *(Wary)*

Well, I like a great many writers; I have a considerable . . .
catholicity of taste, if I may say so. Those two men are fine,
each in his way. *(Warming up)* Baudelaire, of course . . . uh
. . . is by far the finer of the two, but Michener has a place
. . . in our . . . uh . . . national . . .

JERRY

Skip it.

PETER

I . . . sorry.

JERRY

Do you know what I did before I went to the zoo today? I
walked all the way up Fifth Avenue from Washington Square;
all the way.

PETER

Oh; you live in the Village! *(This seems to enlighten* PETER)

JERRY

No, I don't. I took the subway down to the Village so I could
walk all the way up Fifth Avenue to the zoo. It's one of those
things a person has to do; sometimes a person has to go a very
long distance out of his way to come back a short distance
correctly.

PETER (*Almost pouting*)
Oh, I thought you lived in the Village.


JERRY
What were you trying to do? Make sense out of things? Bring order? The old pigeonhole bit? Well, that's easy; I'll tell you. I live in a four-story brownstone roominghouse on the upper West Side between Columbus Avenue and Central Park West. I live on the top floor; rear; west. It's a laughably small room, and one of my walls is made of beaverboard; this beaverboard separates my room from another laughably small room, so I assume that the two rooms were once one room, a small room, but not necessarily laughable. The room beyond my beaverboard wall is occupied by a colored queen who always keeps his door open; well, not always but *always* when he's plucking his eyebrows, which he does with Buddhist concentration. This colored queen has rotten teeth, which is rare, and he has a Japanese kimono, which is also pretty rare; and he wears this kimono to and from the john in the hall, which is pretty frequent. I mean, he goes to the john a lot. He never bothers me, and he never brings anyone up to his room. All he does is pluck his eyebrows, wear his kimono and go to the john. Now, the two front rooms on my floor are a little larger, I guess; but they're pretty small, too. There's a Puerto Rican family in one of them, a husband, a wife, and some kids; I don't know how many. These people entertain a lot. And in the other front room, there's somebody living there, but I don't know who it is. I've never seen who it is. Never. Never ever.


PETER (*Embarrassed*)
Why . . . why do you live there?

JERRY
*(From a distance again)* I don't know.


PETER
It doesn't sound like a very nice place . . . where you live.


JERRY
Well, no; it isn't an apartment in the East Seventies. But, then again, I don't have one wife, two daughters, two cats and two parakeets. What I do have, I have toilet articles, a few clothes, a hot plate that I'm not supposed to have, a can opener, one that works with a key, you know; a knife, two forks, and two spoons, one small, one large; three plates, a cup, a saucer, a drinking glass, two picture frames, both empty, eight or nine books, a pack of pornographic playing cards, regular deck, an old Western Union typewriter that prints nothing but capital letters, and a small strongbox without a lock which has in it . . . what? Rocks! Some rocks . . . sea-rounded rocks I picked up on the beach when I was a kid. Under which . . . weighed down . . . are some letters . . . please letters . . . please why don't you do this, and please when will you do that letters. And when letters, too. When will you write? When will you come? When? These letters are from more recent years.


PETER
*(Stares glumly at his shoes, then)* About those two empty picture frames . . . ?


JERRY
I don't see why they need any explanation at all. Isn't it clear? I don't have pictures of anyone to put in them.

PETER

Your parents . . . perhaps . . . a girl friend . . .

JERRY

You're a very sweet man, and you're possessed of a truly
enviable innocence. But good old Mom and good old Pop are
dead . . . you know? . . . I'm broken up about it, too . . . I
mean really. BUT. That particular vaudeville act is playing
the cloud circuit now, so I don't see how I can look at them,
all neat and framed. Besides, or, rather, to be pointed about
it, good old Mom walked out on good old Pop when I was ten
and a half years old; she embarked on an adulterous turn of
our southern states . . . a journey of a year's duration . . . and
her most constant companion . . . among others, among
many others . . . was a Mr. Barleycorn. At least, that's what
good old Pop told me after he went down . . . came back . . .
brought her body north. We'd received the news between
Christmas and New Year's, you see, that good old Mom had
parted with the ghost in some dump in Alabama. And,
without the ghost . . . she was less welcome. I mean, what
was she? A stiff . . . a northern stiff. At any rate, good old Pop
celebrated the New Year for an even two weeks and then
slapped into the front of a somewhat moving city omnibus,
which sort of cleaned things out family-wise. Well no; then
there was Mom's sister, who was given neither to sin nor the
consolations of the bottle. I moved in on her, and my
memory of her is slight excepting I remember still that she did
all things dourly: sleeping, eating, working, praying. She
dropped dead on the stairs to her apartment, my apartment
then, too, on the afternoon of my high school graduation. A
terribly middle-European joke, if you ask me.

PETER

Oh, my; oh, my.

JERRY

Oh, your what? But that was a long time ago, and I have no feeling about any of it that I care to admit to myself. Perhaps you can see, though, why good old Mom and good old Pop are frameless. What's your name? Your first name?

PETER

I'm Peter.

JERRY

I'd forgotten to ask you. I'm Jerry.

PETER

(With a slight, nervous laugh) Hello, Jerry.

JERRY

(Nods his hello) And let's see now; what's the point of having a girl's picture, especially in two frames? I have two picture frames, you remember. I never see the pretty little ladies more than once, and most of them wouldn't be caught in the same room with a camera. It's odd, and I wonder if it's sad.

PETER

The girls?

JERRY

No. I wonder if it's sad that I never see the little ladies more than once. I've never been able to have sex with, or, how is it put? . . . make love to anybody more than once. Once; that's it. . . . Oh, wait; for a week and a half, when I was fifteen . . . and I hang my head in shame that puberty was late . . . I was a h-o-m-o-s-e-x-u-a-l. I mean, I was queer . . . (Very fast) . . . queer, queer, queer . . . with bells ringing, banners snapping in the wind. And for those eleven days, I met at least twice a day with the park superintendent's son . . . a Greek boy, whose birthday was the same as mine, except he was a year older. I think I was very much in love . . . maybe just with sex. But that was the jazz of a very special hotel, wasn't it? And now; oh, do I love the little ladies; really, I love them. For about an hour.

PETER

Well, it seems perfectly simple to me. . . .

JERRY (*Angry*)

Look! Are you going to tell me to get married and have parakeets?

PETER (*Angry himself*)

Forget the parakeets! And stay single if you want to. It's no business of mine. I didn't start this conversation in the . . .

JERRY

All right, all right. I'm sorry. All right? You're not angry?

PETER (*Laughing*)

No, I'm not angry.

JERRY (*Relieved*)

Good. (*Now back to his previous tone*) Interesting that you asked me about the picture frames. I would have thought that you would have asked me about the pornographic playing cards.

PETER

(*With a knowing smile*) Oh, I've seen those cards.

JERRY

That's not the point. (Laughs) I suppose when you were a kid
you and your pals passed them around, or you had a pack of
your own.

PETER

Well, I guess a lot of us did.

JERRY

And you threw them away just before you got married.

PETER

Oh, now; look here. I didn't *need* anything like that when I
got older.

JERRY

No?

PETER (Embarrassed)

I'd rather not talk about these things.

JERRY

So? Don't. Besides, I· wasn't trying to plumb your post-
adolescent sexual life and hard times; what I wanted to get at is
the value difference between pornographic playing cards
when you're a kid, and pornographic playing cards when
you're older. It's that when you're a kid you use the cards as a
substitute for a real experience, and when you're older you
use real experience as a substitute for the fantasy. But I
imagine you'd rather hear about what happened at the zoo.

PETER (Enthusiastic)

Oh, yes; the zoo. (Then, awkward) That is . . . if you. . . .

JERRY

Let me tell you about why I went . . . well, let me tell you
some things. I've told you about the fourth floor of the
roominghouse where I live. I think the rooms are better as
you go down, floor by floor. I guess they are; I don't know. I
don't know any of the people on the third and second floors.
Oh, wait! I do know that there's a lady living on the third
floor, in the front. I know because she cries all the time.
Whenever I go out or come back in, whenever I pass her
door, I always hear her crying, muffled, but . . . very
determined. Very determined indeed. But the one I'm getting
to, and all about the dog, is the landlady. I don't like to use
words that are too harsh in describing people. I don't like to.
But the landlady is a fat, ugly, mean, stupid, unwashed,
misanthropic, cheap, drunken bag of garbage. And you may
have noticed that I very seldom use profanity, so I can't
describe her as well as I might.


PETER

You describe her . . . vividly.


JERRY

Well, thanks. Anyway, she has a dog, and I will tell you about
the dog, and she and her dog are the gatekeepers of my
dwelling. The woman is bad enough; she leans around in the
entrance hall, spying to see that I don't bring in things or
people, and when she's had her midafternoon pint of lemon-
flavored gin she always stops me in the hall, and grabs ahold
of my coat or my arm, and she presses her disgusting body up
against me to keep me in a corner so she can talk to me. The
smell of her body and her breath . . . you can't imagine it
. . . and somewhere, somewhere in the back of that pea-sized
brain of hers, an organ developed just enough to let her eat,
drink, and emit, she has some foul parody of sexual desire.
And I, Peter, I am the object of her sweaty lust.

PETER

That's disgusting. That's . . . horrible.


JERRY

But I have found a way to keep her off. When she talks to me,
when she presses herself to my body and mumbles about her
room and how I should come there, I merely say: but, Love;
wasn't yesterday enough for you, and the day before? Then
she puzzles, she makes slits of her tiny eyes, she sways a little,
and then, Peter . . . and it is at this moment that I think I
might be doing some good in that tormented house . . . a
simple-minded smile begins to form on her unthinkable face,
and she giggles and groans as she thinks about yesterday and
the day before; as she believes and relives what never
happened. Then, she motions to that black monster of a dog
she has, and she goes back to her room. And I am safe until
our next meeting.


PETER

It's so . . . unthinkable. I find it hard to believe that people
such as that really *are*.


JERRY

(*Lightly mocking*) It's for reading about, isn't it?

PETER (*Seriously*)

Yes.


JERRY

And fact is better left to fiction. You're right, Peter. Well,
what I have been meaning to tell you about is the dog; I shall,
now.

PETER *(Nervously)*
Oh, yes; the dog.


JERRY
Don't go. You're not thinking of going, are you?


PETER
Well . . . no, I don't think so.


JERRY
*(As if to a child)* Because after I tell you about the dog, do you
know what then? Then . . . then I'll tell you about what
happened at the zoo.


PETER *(Laughing faintly)*
You're . . . you're full of stories, aren't you?


JERRY
You don't *have* to listen. Nobody is holding you here;
remember that. Keep that in your mind.


PETER *(Irritably)*
I know that.


JERRY
You do? Good.
> *(The following long speech, it seems to me, should be
> done with a great deal of action, to achieve a hypnotic
> effect on Peter, and on the audience, too. Some
> specific actions have been suggested, but the director
> and the actor playing Jerry might best work it out for
> themselves)*

ALL RIGHT. (As if reading from a huge billboard) THE
STORY OF JERRY AND THE DOG! (Natural again)
What I am going to tell you has something to do with how
sometimes it's necessary to go a long distance out of the way in
order to come back a short distance correctly; or, maybe I only
think that it has something to do with that. But, it's why I
went to the zoo today, and why I walked north . . . northerly,
rather . . . until I came here. All right. The dog, I think I told
you, is a black monster of a beast: an oversized head, tiny,
tiny ears, and eyes . . . bloodshot, infected, maybe; and a
body you can see the ribs through the skin. The dog is black,
all black; all black except for the bloodshot eyes, and . . . yes
. . . and an open sore on its . . . right forepaw; that is red,
too. And, oh yes; the poor monster, and I do believe it's an
old dog . . . it's certainly a misused one . . . almost always
has an erection . . . of sorts. That's red, too. And . . . what
else? . . . oh, yes; there's a gray-yellow-white color, too, when
he bares his fangs. Like this: Grrrrrrr! Which is what he did
when he saw me for the first time . . . the day I moved in. I
worried about that animal the very first minute I met him.
Now, animals don't take to me like Saint Francis had birds
hanging off him all the time. What I mean is: animals are
indifferent to me . . . like people (He smiles slightly) . . .
most of the time. But this dog wasn't indifferent. From the
very beginning he'd snarl and then go for me, to get one of my
legs. Not like he was rabid, you know; he was sort of a stumbly
dog, but he wasn't half-assed, either. It was a good, stumbly
run; but I always got away. He got a piece of my trouser leg,
look, you can see right here, where it's mended; he got that
the second day I lived there; but, I kicked free and got upstairs
fast, so that was that. (Puzzles) I still don't know to this day
how the other roomers manage it, but you know what I think:
I think it had to do only with me. Cozy. So. Anyway, this
went on for over a week, whenever I came in; but never when
I went out. That's funny. Or, it was funny. I could pack up

and live in the street for all the dog cared. Well, I thought about it up in my room one day, one of the times after I'd bolted upstairs, and I made up my mind. I decided: First, I'll kill the dog with kindness, and if that doesn't work . . . I'll just kill him. (PETER *winces*) Don't react, Peter; just listen. So, the next day I went out and bought a bag of hamburgers, medium rare, no catsup, no onion; and on the way home I threw away all the rolls and kept just the meat.

*(Action for the following, perhaps)*
When I got back to the roominghouse the dog was waiting for me. I half opened the door that led into the entrance hall, and there he was; waiting for me. It figured. I went in, very cautiously, and I had the hamburgers, you remember; I opened the bag, and I set the meat down about twelve feet from where the dog was snarling at me. Like so! He snarled; stopped snarling; sniffed; moved slowly; then faster; then faster toward the meat. Well, when he got to it he stopped, and he looked at me. I smiled; but tentatively, you understand. He turned his face back to the hamburgers, smelled, sniffed some more, and then . . . RRRAAAAGGGGGHHHH, like that . . . he tore into them. It was as if he had never eaten anything in his life before, except like garbage. Which might very well have been the truth. I don't think the landlady ever eats anything but garbage. But. He ate all the hamburgers, almost all at once, making sounds in his throat like a woman. *Then*, when he'd finished the meat, the hamburger, and tried to eat the paper, too, he sat down and smiled. I think he smiled; I know cats do. It was a very gratifying few moments. Then, BAM, he snarled and made for me again. He didn't get me this time, either. So, I got upstairs, and I lay down on my bed and started to think about the dog again. To be truthful, I was offended, and I was damn mad, too. It was six perfectly good hamburgers with not enough pork in them to make it disgusting. I was offended. But, after a while, I decided to try it for a few more days. If you think about it, this dog had what

amounted to an antipathy toward me; really. And, I wondered
if I mightn't overcome this antipathy. So, I tried it for five
more days, but it was always the same: snarl; sniff; move;
faster; stare; gobble; RAAGGGHHH; smile; snarl; BAM.
Well, now; by this time Columbus Avenue was strewn with
hamburger rolls and I was less offended than disgusted. So, I
decided to kill the dog.

      (PETER *raises a hand in protest*)
Oh, don't be so alarmed, Peter; I didn't succeed. The day I
tried to kill the dog I bought only one hamburger and what I
thought was a murderous portion of rat poison. When I
bought the hamburger I asked the man not to bother with the
roll, all I wanted was the meat. I expected some reaction from
him, like: we don't sell no hamburgers without rolls; or, wha'
d'ya wanna do, eat it out'a ya han's? But no; he smiled
benignly, wrapped up the hamburger in waxed paper, and
said: A bite for ya pussy-cat? I wanted to say: No, not really;
it's part of a plan to poison a dog I know. But, you can't say "a
dog I know" without sounding funny; so I said, a little too
loud, I'm afraid, and too formally: YES, A BITE FOR MY
PUSSY-CAT. People looked up. It always happens when I try
to simplify things; people look up. But that's neither hither
nor thither. So. On my way back to the roominghouse, I
kneaded the hamburger and the rat poison together between
my hands, at that point feeling as much sadness as disgust. I
opened the door to the entrance hall, and there the monster
was, waiting to take the offering and then jump me. Poor
bastard; he never learned that the moment he took to smile
before he went for me gave me time enough to get out of
range. BUT, there he was; malevolence with an erection,
waiting. I put the poison patty down, moved toward the stairs
and watched. The poor animal gobbled the food down as
usual, smiled, which made me almost sick, and then, BAM.
But, I sprinted up the stairs, as usual, and the dog didn't get
me, as usual. AND IT CAME TO PASS THAT THE

BEAST WAS DEATHLY ILL. I knew this because he no longer attended me, and because the landlady sobered up. She stopped me in the hall the same evening of the attempted murder and confided the information that God had struck her puppy-dog a surely fatal blow. She had forgotten her bewildered lust, and her eyes were wide open for the first time. They looked like the dog's eyes. She sniveled and implored me to pray for the animal. I wanted to say to her: Madam, I have myself to pray for, the colored queen, the Puerto Rican family, the person in the front room whom I've never seen, the woman who cries deliberately behind her closed door, and the rest of the people in all roominghouses, everywhere; besides, Madam, I don't understand how to pray. But . . . to simplify things . . . I told her I would pray. She looked up. She said that I was a liar, and that I probably wanted the dog to die. I told her, and there was so much truth here, that I didn't want the dog to die. I didn't, and not just because I'd poisoned him. I'm afraid that I must tell you I wanted the dog to live so that I could see what our new relationship might come to.

> (PETER *indicates his increasing displeasure and slowly growing antagonism*)

Please understand, Peter; that sort of thing is important. You must believe me; it *is* important. We have to know the effect of our actions. (*Another deep sigh*) Well, anyway; the dog recovered. I have no idea why, unless he was a descendant of the puppy that guarded the gates of hell or some such resort. I'm not up on my mythology. (*He pronounces the word myth-o-logy*) Are you?

> (PETER *sets to thinking, but* JERRY *goes on*)

At any rate, and you've missed the eight-thousand-dollar question, Peter; at any rate, the dog recovered his health and the landlady recovered her thirst, in no way altered by the bow-wow's deliverance. When I came home from a movie that was playing on Forty-second Street, a movie I'd seen, or

one that was very much like one or several I'd seen, after the
landlady told me puppykins was better, I was so hoping for the
dog to be waiting for me. I was . . . well, how would you put
it . . . enticed? . . . fascinated? . . . no, I don't think so . . .
heart-shatteringly anxious, that's it; I was heart-shatteringly
anxious to confront my friend again.
    (PETER *reacts scoffingly*)
Yes, Peter; friend. That's the only word for it. I was heart-
shatteringly et cetera to confront my doggy friend again. I
came in the door and advanced, unafraid, to the center of the
entrance hall. The beast was there . . . looking at me. And,
you know, he looked better for his scrape with the nevermind.
I stopped; I looked at him; he looked at me. I think . . . I
think we stayed a long time that way . . . still, stone-statue
. . . just looking at one another. I looked more into his face
than he looked into mine. I mean, I can concentrate longer at
looking into a dog's face than a dog can concentrate at looking
into mine, or into anybody else's face, for that matter. But
during that twenty seconds or two hours that we looked into
each other's face, we made contact. Now, here is what I had
wanted to happen: I loved the dog now, and I wanted him to
love me. I had tried to love, and I had tried to kill, and both
had been unsuccessful by themselves. I hoped . . . and I don't
really know why I expected the dog to understand anything,
much less my motivations . . . I hoped that the dog would
understand.
    (PETER *seems to be hypnotized*)
It's just . . . it's just that . . . (JERRY *is abnormally tense,
now*) . . . it's just that if you can't deal with people, you have
to make a start somewhere. WITH ANIMALS! (*Much faster
now, and like a conspirator*) Don't you see? A person has to
have some way of dealing with SOMETHING. If not with
people . . . if not with people . . . SOMETHING. With a
bed, with a cockroach, with a mirror . . . no, that's too hard,
that's one of the last steps. With a cockroach, with a . . . with

a . . . with a carpet, a roll of toilet paper . . . no, not that,
either . . . that's a mirror, too; always check bleeding. You
see how hard it is to find things? With a street corner, and too
many lights, all colors reflecting on the oily-wet streets . . .
with a wisp of smoke, a wisp . . . of smoke . . . with . . . with
pornographic playing cards, with a strongbox . . . WITH-
OUT A LOCK . . . with love, with vomiting, with crying,
with fury because the pretty little ladies aren't pretty little
ladies, with making money with your body which is an act of
love and I could prove it, with howling because you're alive;
with God. How about that? WITH GOD WHO IS A
COLORED QUEEN WHO WEARS A KIMONO AND
PLUCKS HIS EYEBROWS, WHO IS A WOMAN WHO
CRIES WITH DETERMINATION BEHIND HER
CLOSED DOOR . . . with God who, I'm told, turned his
back on the whole thing some time ago . . . with . . . some
day, with people. (JERRY *sighs the next word heavily*) People.
With an idea; a concept. And where better, where ever better
in this humiliating excuse for a jail, where better to commu-
nicate one single, simple-minded idea than in an entrance
hall? Where? It would be A START! Where better to make a
beginning . . . to understand and just possibly be understood
. . . a beginning of an understanding, than with . . .
>       (Here JERRY *seems to fall into almost grotesque
>       fatigue*)
. . . than with A DOG. Just that; a dog.
>       (Here there is a silence that might be prolonged for a
>       moment or so; then JERRY *wearily finishes his story*)
A dog. It seemed like a perfectly sensible idea. Man is a dog's
best friend, remember. So: the dog and I looked at each other.
I longer than the dog. And what I saw then has been the same
ever since. Whenever the dog and I see each other we both
stop where we are. We regard each other with a mixture of
sadness and suspicion, and then we feign indifference. We
walk past each other safely; we have an understanding. It's

very sad, but you'll have to admit that it is an understanding.
We had made many attempts at contact, and we had failed.
The dog has returned to garbage, and I to solitary but free
passage. I have not returned. I mean to say, I have *gained*
solitary free passage, if that much further loss can be said to be
gain. I have learned that neither kindness nor cruelty by
themselves, independent of each other, creates any effect
beyond themselves; and I have learned that the two com-
bined, together, at the same time, are the teaching emotion.
And what is gained is loss. And what has been the result: the
dog and I have attained a compromise; more of a bargain,
really. We neither love nor hurt because we do not try to
reach each other. And, *was* trying to feed the dog an act of
love? And, perhaps, was the dog's attempt to bite me *not* an
act of love? If we can so misunderstand, well then, why have
we invented the word love in the first place?

    *(There is silence.)*
The Story of Jerry and the Dog: the end.

    (PETER *is silent*)
Well, Peter?(JERRY *is suddenly cheerful*) Well, Peter? Do you
think I could sell that story to the *Reader's Digest* and make a
couple of hundred bucks for *The Most Unforgettable Charac-
ter I've Ever Met?* Huh?

    (JERRY *is animated, but* PETER *is disturbed*)
Oh, come on now, Peter; tell me what you think.


            PETER *(Numb)*
I . . . I don't understand what . . . I don't think I . . . *(Now,
almost tearfully)* Why did you tell me all of this?


            JERRY
Why not?


            PETER
I DON'T UNDERSTAND!

JERRY
*(Furious, but whispering)* That's a lie.

PETER
No. No, it's not.

JERRY *(Quietly)*
I tried to explain it to you as I went along. I went slowly; it all has to do with . . .

PETER
I DON'T WANT TO HEAR ANY MORE. I don't under-stand you, or your landlady, or her dog. . . .

JERRY
*Her* dog! I thought it was my . . . No. No, you're right. It *is* her dog. *(Looks at* PETER *intently, shaking his head)* I don't know what I was thinking about; of course you don't understand. *(In a monotone, wearily)* I don't live in your block; I'm not married to two parakeets, or whatever your setup is. I am a *permanent transient,* and my home is the sickening roominghouses on the West Side of New York City, which is the greatest city in the world. Amen.

PETER
I'm . . . I'm sorry; I didn't mean to . . .

JERRY
Forget it. I suppose you don't quite know what to make of me, eh?

PETER *(A joke)*
We get all kinds in publishing. *(Chuckles)*

JERRY

You're a funny man. *(He forces a laugh)* You know that?
You're a very . . . a richly comic person.


PETER

*(Modestly, but amused)* Oh, now, not really. *(Still chuckling)*


JERRY

Peter, do I annoy you, or confuse you?


PETER *(Lightly)*

Well, I must confess that this wasn't the kind of afternoon I'd
anticipated.


JERRY

You mean, I'm not the gentleman you were expecting.


PETER

I wasn't expecting anybody.


JERRY

No, I don't imagine you were. But I'm here, and I'm not
leaving.


PETER

*(Consulting his watch)* Well, you may not be, but I must be
getting home now.


JERRY

Oh, come on; stay a while longer.


PETER

I really should get home; you see . . .

JERRY
(*Tickles* PETER's *ribs with his fingers*) Oh, come on.


PETER
(*He is very ticklish; as* JERRY *continues to tickle him his voice becomes falsetto*)
No, I . . . OHHHHH! Don't do that. Stop, Stop. Ohhh, no, no.


JERRY
Oh, come on.


PETER
(*As* JERRY *tickles*) Oh, hee, hee, hee. I must go. I . . . hee, hee, hee. After all, stop, stop, hee, hee, hee, after all, the parakeets will be getting dinner ready soon. Hee, hee. And the cats are setting the table. Stop, stop, and, and . . . (PETER *is beside himself now*) . . . and we're having . . . hee, hee . . . uh . . . ho, ho, ho.
> (JERRY *stops tickling* PETER, *but the combination of the tickling and his own mad whimsy has* PETER *laughing almost hysterically. As his laughter continues, then subsides,* JERRY *watches him, with a curious fixed smile*). JERRY *moves to* PETER's *bench and sits down beside him. This is the first time* JERRY *has sat down during the play*)


JERRY
Peter?


PETER
Oh, ha, ha, ha, ha, ha. What? What?


JERRY
Listen, now.

PETER
Oh, ho, ho. What . . . what is it, Jerry? Oh, my.

JERRY *(Mysteriously)*
Peter, do you want to know what happened at the zoo?

PETER
Ah, ha, ha. The what? Oh, yes; the zoo. Oh, ho, ho. Well, I
had my own zoo there for a moment with . . . hee, hee, the
parakeets getting dinner ready, and the . . . ha, ha, whatever
it was, the . . .

JERRY *(Calmly)*
Yes, that was very funny, Peter. I wouldn't have expected it.
But do you want to hear about what happened at the zoo, or
not?

PETER
Yes. Yes, by all means; tell me what happened at the zoo.
Oh, my. I don't know what happened to me.

JERRY
Now I'll let you in on what happened at the zoo; but first, I
should tell you why I went to the zoo. I went to the zoo to find
out more about the way people exist with animals, and the
way animals exist with each other, and with people too. It
probably wasn't a fair test, what with everyone separated by
bars from everyone else, the animals for the most part from
each other, and always the people from the animals. But, if
it's a zoo, that's the way it is. *(He pokes* PETER *on the arm)*
Move over.

PETER *(Friendly)*
I'm sorry, haven't you enough room? *(He shifts a little)*

JERRY *(Smiling slightly)*
Well, all the animals are there, and all the people are there,
and it's Sunday and all the children are there. *(He pokes
PETER again)* Move over.


PETER
*(Patiently, still friendly)* All right.
  *(He moves some more, and JERRY has all the room he
  might need)*


JERRY
And it's a hot day, so all the stench is there, too, and all the
balloon sellers, and all the ice cream sellers, and all the seals
are barking, and all the birds are screaming. *(Pokes PETER
harder)* Move over!


PETER
*(Beginning to be annoyed)* Look here, you have more than
enough room! *(But he moves more, and is now fairly cramped
at one end of the bench)*


JERRY
And I am there, and it's feeding time at the lions' house, and
the lion keeper comes into the lion cage, one of the lion
cages, to feed one of the lions. *(Punches PETER on the arm,
hard)* MOVE OVER!


PETER
*(Very annoyed)* I can't move over any more, and stop hitting
me. What's the matter with you?


JERRY
Do you want to hear the story? *(Punches PETER's arm again)*

PETER *(Flabbergasted)*

I'm not so sure! I certainly don't want to be punched in the arm.

JERRY

*(Punches* PETER's *arm again)* Like that?

PETER

Stop it! What's the matter with you?

JERRY

I'm crazy, you bastard.

PETER

That isn't funny.

JERRY

Listen to me, Peter. I want this bench. You go sit on the bench over there, and if you're good I'll tell you the rest of the story.

PETER *(Flustered)*

But . . . whatever for? What *is* the matter with you? Besides, I see no reason why I should give up this bench. I sit on this bench almost every Sunday afternoon, in good weather. It's secluded here; there's never anyone sitting here, so I have it all to myself.

JERRY *(Softly)*

Get off this bench, Peter; I want it.

PETER

*(Almost whining)* No.

JERRY

I said I want this bench, and I'm going to have it. Now get over there.

PETER

People can't have everything they want. You should know that; it's a rule; people can have some of the things they want, but they can't have everything.

JERRY *(Laughs)*

Imbecile! You're slow-witted!

PETER

Stop that!

JERRY

You're a vegetable! Go lie down on the ground.

PETER *(Intense)*

Now *you* listen to me. I've put up with you all afternoon.

JERRY

Not really.

PETER

LONG ENOUGH. I've put up with you long enough. I've listened to you because you seemed . . . well, because I thought you wanted to talk to somebody.

JERRY

You put things well; economically, and, yet . . . oh, what is the word I want to put justice to your . . . JESUS, you make me sick . . . get off here and give me my bench.

PETER

MY BENCH!


JERRY

(Pushes PETER *almost, but not quite, off the bench*) Get out of
my sight.


PETER

(*Regaining his position*) God da . . . mn you. That's enough!
I've had enough of you. I will not give up this bench; you
can't have it, and that's that. Now, go away.
            (JERRY *snorts but does not move*)
Go away, I said.
            (JERRY *does not move*)
Get away from here. If you don't move on . . . you're a bum
. . . that's what you are. . . . If you don't move on, I'll get a
policeman here and make you go.
            (JERRY *laughs, stays*)
I warn you, I'll call a policeman.


JERRY *(Softly)*

You won't find a policeman around here; they're all over on
the west side of the park chasing fairies down from trees or
out of the bushes. That's all they do. That's their
function. So scream your head off; it won't do you any
good.


PETER

POLICE! I warn you, I'll have you arrested. POLICE!
(*Pause*) I said POLICE! (*Pause*) I feel ridiculous.


JERRY

You look ridiculous: a grown man screaming for the police on

a bright Sunday afternoon in the park with nobody harming
you. If a policeman *did* fill his quota and come sludging over
this way he'd probably take you in as a nut.

PETER
(*With disgust and impotence*) Great God, I just came here to
read, and now you want me to give up the bench. You're
mad.

JERRY
Hey, I got news for you, as they say. I'm on your precious
bench, and you're never going to have it for yourself again.

PETER (*Furious*)
Look, you; get off my bench. I don't care if it makes any sense
or not. I want this bench to myself; I want you OFF IT!

JERRY (*Mocking*)
Aw . . . look who's mad.

PETER
GET OUT!

JERRY
No.

PETER
I WARN YOU!

JERRY
Do you know how ridiculous you look *now?*

PETER

*(His fury and self-consciousness have possessed him)* It doesn't matter. *(He is almost crying)* GET AWAY FROM MY BENCH!

JERRY

Why? You have everything in the world you want; you've told me about your home, and your family, and *your own* little zoo. You have everything, and now you want this bench. Are these the things men fight for? Tell me, Peter, is this bench, this iron and this wood, is this your honor? Is this the thing in the world you'd fight for? Can you think of anything more absurd?

PETER

Absurd? Look, I'm not going to talk to you about honor, or even try to explain it to you. Besides, it isn't a question of honor; but even if it were, you wouldn't understand.

JERRY *(Contemptuously)*

You don't even know what you're saying, do you? This is probably the first time in your life you've had anything more trying to face than changing your cats' toilet box. Stupid! Don't you have any idea, not even the slightest, what other people *need*?

PETER

Oh, boy, listen to you; well, you don't need this bench. That's for sure.

JERRY

Yes; yes, I do.

PETER (*Quivering*)

I've come here for years; I have hours of great pleasure, great satisfaction, right here. And that's important to a man. I'm a responsible person, and I'm a GROWNUP. This is my bench, and you have no right to take it away from me.

JERRY

Fight for it, then. Defend yourself; defend your bench.

PETER

You've *pushed* me to it. Get up and fight.

JERRY

Like a man?

PETER (*Still angry*)

Yes, like a man, if you insist on mocking me even further.

JERRY

I'll have to give you credit for one thing: you *are* a vegetable, and a slightly nearsighted one, I think . . .

PETER

THAT'S ENOUGH. . . .

JERRY

. . . but, you know, as they say on TV all the time—you know—and I mean this, Peter, you have a certain dignity; it surprises me. . . .

PETER

STOP!

JERRY

*(Rises lazily)* Very well, Peter, we'll battle for the bench, but we're not evenly matched.

*(He takes out and clicks open an ugly-looking knife)*

PETER

*(Suddenly awakening to the reality of the situation)*
You *are* mad! You're stark raving mad! YOU'RE GOING TO KILL ME!

*(But before* PETER *has time to think what to do,* JERRY *tosses the knife at* PETER's *feet)*

JERRY

There you go. Pick it up. You have the knife and we'll be more evenly matched.

PETER *(Horrified)*

No!

JERRY

*(Rushes over to* PETER, *grabs him by the collar;* PETER *rises; their faces almost touch)*
Now you pick up that knife and you fight with me. You fight for your self-respect; you fight for that goddamned bench.

PETER *(Struggling)*
No! Let . . . let go of me! He . . . Help!

JERRY

*(Slaps* PETER *on each "fight")* You fight, you miserable bastard; fight for that bench; fight for your parakeets; fight for your cats, fight for your two daughters; fight for your wife; fight for your manhood, you pathetic little vegetable. *(Spits in*

PETER's *face)* You couldn't even get your wife with a male
child.


PETER

*(Breaks away, enraged)* It's a matter of genetics, not manhood, you . . . you monster.
> *(He darts down, picks up the knife and backs off a*
> *little; he is breathing heavily)*
I'll give you one last chance; get out of here and leave me
alone!
> *(He holds the knife with a firm arm, but far in front of*
> *him, not to attack, but to defend)*


JERRY *(Sighs heavily)*

So be it!
> *(With a rush he charges* PETER *and impales himself on*
> *the knife. Tableau: For just a moment, complete*
> *silence,* JERRY *impaled on the knife at the end of*
> PETER's *still firm arm. Then* PETER *screams, pulls*
> *away, leaving the knife in* JERRY. JERRY *is motionless,*
> *on point. Then he, too, screams, and it must be the*
> *sound of an infuriated and fatally wounded animal.*
> *With the knife in him, he stumbles back to the bench*
> *that* PETER *had vacated. He crumbles there, sitting,*
> *facing* PETER, *his eyes wide in agony, his mouth open)*


PETER *(Whispering)*

Oh my God, oh my God, oh my God. . . .
> *(He repeats these words many times, very rapidly)*


JERRY

> *(*JERRY *is dying; but now his expression seems to*
> *change. His features relax, and while his voice varies,*

*sometimes wrenched with pain, for the most part he
seems removed from his dying. He smiles)*
Thank you, Peter. I mean that, now; thank you very much.
(PETER's *mouth drops open. He cannot move; he is
transfixed)*
Oh, Peter, I was so afraid I'd drive you away. *(He laughs as
best he can)* You don't know how afraid I was you'd go away
and leave me. Well, here we are. You see? Here we *are. . . .*
Peter? . . . Peter . . . thank you. I came unto you *(He laughs,
so faintly)* and you have comforted me. Dear Peter.


PETER

*(Almost fainting)* Oh my God!


JERRY

You'd better go now. Somebody might come by, and you
don't want to be here when anyone comes.


PETER

*(Does not move, but begins to weep)*
Oh my God, oh my God.


JERRY

*(Most faintly, now; he is very near death)*
You won't be coming back here any more, Peter; you've been
dispossessed. You've lost your bench, but you've defended
your honor. And Peter, I'll tell you something now; you're not
really a vegetable; it's all right, you're an animal. You're an
animal, too. But you'd better hurry now, Peter. Hurry, you'd
better go . . . see?
(JERRY *takes a handkerchief and with great effort and
pain wipes the knife handle clean of fingerprints)*
Hurry away, Peter.
(PETER *begins to stagger away)*

Wait . . . wait, Peter. Take your book . . . book. Right here
. . . beside me . . . on your bench . . . my bench, rather.
Come . . . take your book.
         (PETER *starts for the book, but retreats*)
Hurry . . . Peter.
         (PETER *rushes to the bench, grabs the book, retreats*)
Very good, Peter . . . very good. Now . . . hurry away.
         (PETER *hesitates for a moment, then flees, stage-left*)
Hurry away. . . . (*His eyes are closed now*) Hurry away, your
parakeets are making the dinner . . . the cats . . . are setting
the table . . .


                    PETER (*Off stage*)
         (*A pitiful howl*)
OH MY GOD!


                         JERRY
         (*His eyes still closed, he shakes his head and speaks; a
         combination of scornful mimicry and supplication*)
Oh . . . my . . . God.
         (*He is dead*)

                    CURTAIN

# The Death
# of Bessie Smith

A PLAY IN EIGHT SCENES (1959)

*For Ned Rorem*

FIRST PERFORMANCE
April 21, 1960, Berlin, Germany.

Schlosspark Theater.

# THE PLAYERS

### BERNIE

A Negro, about forty, thin.

### JACK

A dark-skinned Negro, forty-five, bulky, with a deep voice and a mustache.

### THE FATHER

A thin, balding white man, about fifty-five.

### THE NURSE

A southern white girl, full blown, dark or red-haired, pretty, with a wild laugh. Twenty-six.

### THE ORDERLY

A light-skinned Negro, twenty-eight, clean-shaven, trim, prim.

### SECOND NURSE

A southern white girl, blond, not too pretty, about thirty.

### THE INTERN

A southern white man, blond, well put-together, with an amiable face; thirty.

## THE SCENE

*Afternoon and early evening, September 26, 1937. In and around the city of Memphis, Tennessee.*

## THE SET

*The set for this play will vary, naturally, as stages vary—from theatre to theatre. So, the suggestions put down below, while they might serve as a useful guide, are but a general idea— what the author "sees."*

*What the author "sees" is this: The central and front area of the stage reserved for the admissions room of a hospital, for this is where the major portion of the action of the play takes place. The admissions desk and chair stage-center, facing the audience. A door, leading outside, stage-right; a door, leading to further areas of the hospital, stage-left. Very little more: a bench, perhaps; a chair or two. Running along the rear of the stage, and perhaps a bit on the sides, there should be a raised platform, on which, at various locations, against just the most minimal suggestions of sets, the other scenes of the play are performed. All of this very open, for the whole back wall of the stage is full of the sky, which will vary from scene to scene: a hot blue; a sunset; a great, red-orange-yellow sunset. Sometimes full, sometimes but a hint.*

*At the curtain, let the entire stage be dark against the sky, which is a hot blue. MUSIC against this, for a moment or so, fading to under as the lights come up on:*

## SCENE ONE

*The corner of a barroom.* BERNIE *seated at a table, a beer before him, with glass.* JACK *enters, tentatively, a beer bottle in his hand; he does not see* BERNIE.

BERNIE
*(Recognizing* JACK; *with pleased surprise)* Hey!

JACK
Hm?

BERNIE
Hey; Jack!

JACK
Hm? . . . What? . . . *(Recognizes him)* Bernie!

BERNIE
What you doin' here, boy? C'mon, sit down.

JACK
Well, I'll be damned. . . .

BERNIE
C'mon, sit down, Jack.

JACK

Yeah . . . sure . . . well, I'll be damned. *(Moves over to the table; sits)* Bernie. My God, it's hot. How you been, boy?

BERNIE

Fine; fine. What you *doin'* here?

JACK

Oh, travelin'; travelin'.

BERNIE

On the move, hunh? Boy, you are the last person I expected t'walk in that door; small world, hunh?

JACK

Yeah; yeah.

BERNIE

On the move, hunh? Where you goin'?

JACK

*(Almost, but not quite, mysterious)* North.

BERNIE *(Laughs)*

North! North? That's a big place, friend: north.

JACK

Yeah . . . yeah, it is that: a big place.

BERNIE

*(After a pause; laughs again)* Well, *where,* boy? North *where?*

JACK

(*Coyly; proudly*) New York.


BERNIE

New York!


JACK

Unh-hunh; unh-hunh.


BERNIE

New York, hunh? Well. What you got goin' up there?


JACK

(*Coy again*) Oh . . . well . . . I got somethin' goin' up there.
What *you* been up to, boy?


BERNIE

New York, hunh?


JACK

(*Obviously dying to tell about it*) Unh-hunh.


BERNIE

(*Knowing it*) Well, now, isn't that somethin'. Hey! You want
a beer? You want another beer?


JACK

No, I gotta get . . . well, I don't know, I . . .


BERNIE

(*Rising from the table*) Sure you do. Hot like this? You need a
beer or two, cool you off.

JACK
*(Settling back)* Yeah; why not? Sure, Bernie.


BERNIE
*(A dollar bill in his hand; moving off)* I'll get us a pair. New York, hunh? What's it all about, Jack? Hunh?


JACK *(Chuckles)*
Ah, you'd be surprised, boy; you'd be surprised.
*(Lights fade on this scene, come up on another, which is)*


## SCENE TWO

*Part of a screened-in porch; some wicker furniture, a little the worse for wear.*
*The* NURSE'S FATHER *is seated on the porch, a cane by his chair. Music, loud, from a phonograph, inside.*


FATHER
*(The music is too loud; he grips the arms of his chair; finally)*
Stop it! Stop it! Stop it! Stop it!


NURSE *(From inside)*
What? What did you say?


FATHER
STOP IT!


NURSE
*(Appearing, dressed for duty)* I can't hear you; what do you want?

FATHER

Turn it off! Turn that goddam music off!


NURSE

Honestly, Father . . .


FATHER

Turn it off!
> *(The* NURSE *turns wearily, goes back inside. Music stops)*

Goddam nigger records. *(To* NURSE, *inside)* I got a headache.


NURSE *(Re-entering)*

What?


FATHER

I said, I got a headache; you play those goddam records all the time; blast my head off; you play those goddam nigger records full blast . . . me with a headache. . . .


NURSE *(Wearily)*

You take your pill?


FATHER

No!


NURSE *(Turning)*

I'll get you your pills. . . .


FATHER

I don't want 'em!

NURSE *(Overpatiently)*
All right; then I won't get you your pills.


FATHER
*(After a pause; quietly, petulantly)* You play those goddam records all the time. . . .


NURSE *(Impatiently)*
I'm sorry, Father; I didn't know you had your headache.


FATHER
Don't you use that tone with me!


NURSE
*(With that tone)* I wasn't using any tone. . . .


FATHER
Don't argue!


NURSE
I am not arguing; I don't *want* to argue; it's too *hot* to argue. *(Pause; then quietly)* I don't see why a person can't play a couple of records around here without . . .


FATHER
Damn noise! That's all it is; damn noise.


NURSE
*(After a pause)* I don't suppose you'll drive me to work. I don't suppose, with your headache, you feel up to driving me to the hospital.

FATHER

No.


NURSE

I didn't think you would. And I suppose *you're* going to need the car, too.


FATHER

Yes.


NURSE

Yes; I figured you would. What are you going to do, Father? Are you going to sit here all afternoon on the porch, with your headache, and *watch* the car? Are you going to sit here and watch it all afternoon? You going to sit here with a shotgun and make sure the birds don't crap on it . . . or something?


FATHER

I'm going to need it.


NURSE

Yeah; sure.


FATHER

I said, I'm going to need it.


NURSE

Yeah . . . I heard you. You're going to need it.


FATHER

I am!

NURSE

Yeah; no doubt. You going to drive down to the Democratic Club, and sit around with that bunch of loafers? You going to play big politician today? Hunh?

FATHER

That's enough, now.

NURSE

You going to go down there with that bunch of bums . . . light up one of those expensive cigars, which you have no business smoking, which you can't afford, which *I* cannot afford, to put it more accurately . . . the same brand His Honor the mayor smokes . . . you going to sit down there and talk big, about how you and the mayor are like *this* . . . you going to pretend you're something more than you really are, which is nothing but . . .

FATHER

You be quiet, you!

NURSE

. . . a hanger-on . . . a flunky . . .

FATHER

YOU BE QUIET!

NURSE *(Faster)*

Is that what you need the car for, Father, and I am going to have to take that hot, stinking bus to the hospital?

FATHER

I said, quiet! *(Pause)* I'm sick and tired of hearing you disparage my friendship with the mayor.

NURSE *(Contemptuous)*

Friendship!

FATHER

That's right: friendship.

NURSE

I'll tell you what I'll do: Now that we have His Honor, the mayor, as a patient . . . when I get down to the hospital . . . if I ever get there on that damn bus . . . I'll pay him a call, and I'll just *ask* him about your "friendship" with him; I'll just . . .

FATHER

Don't you go disturbing him; you hear me?

NURSE

Why, I should think the mayor would be *delighted* if the daughter of one of his closest friends was to . . .

FATHER

You're going to make trouble!

NURSE *(Heavily sarcastic)*

Oh, how could I make trouble, Father?

FATHER

You be careful.

NURSE

Oh, that must be quite a friendship. Hey, I got a good idea: you could drive me down to the hospital and you could pay a visit to your good friend the mayor at the same time. Now, *that* is a good idea.

FATHER

Leave off! Just leave off!

NURSE

(*Under her breath*) You make me sick.

FATHER

What! What was that?

NURSE (*Very quietly*)

I said, you make me sick, Father.

FATHER

Yeah? Yeah?
(*He takes his cane, raps it against the floor several times. This gesture, beginning in anger, alters, as it becomes weaker, to a helpless and pathetic flailing; eventually it subsides; the* NURSE *watches it all quietly*)

NURSE (*Tenderly*)

Are you done?

FATHER

Go away; go to work.

NURSE
I'll get you your pills before I go.

FATHER *(Tonelessly)*
I said, I don't want them.

NURSE
I don't care whether you *want* them, or not. . . .

FATHER
I'm not one of your patients!

NURSE
Oh, and aren't I glad you're not.

FATHER
You give them better attention than you give me!

NURSE *(Wearily)*
I don't have patients, Father; I am not a floor nurse; will you get that into your head? I am on admissions; I am on the admissions desk. You *know* that; why do you pretend otherwise?

FATHER
If you were a . . . what-do-you-call-it . . . if you were a floor nurse . . . if you *were*, you'd give your patients better attention than you give me.

NURSE
What *are* you, Father? What are you? Are you sick, or not?

Are you a . . . a . . . a poor cripple, or are you planning to
get yourself up out of that chair, after I go to work, and drive
yourself down to the Democratic Club and sit around with
that bunch of loafers? Make up your mind, Father; you can't
have it every which way.

FATHER

Never mind.

NURSE

You can't; you just can't.

FATHER

Never mind, now!

NURSE

(After a pause) Well, I gotta get to work.

FATHER (Sneering)

Why don't you get your boy friend to drive you to work?

NURSE

All right; leave off.

FATHER

Why don't you get him to come by and pick you up, hunh?

NURSE

I said, leave off!

FATHER

Or is he only interested in driving you back here at night . . .

when it's nice and dark; when it's plenty dark for messing around in his car? Is that it? Why don't you bring him here and let *me* have a look at him; why don't you let me get a look at him some time?

NURSE *(Angry)*
Well, Father . . . *(A very brief gesture at the surroundings)* maybe it's because I don't want him to get a . . .

FATHER
I hear you; I hear you at night; I hear you gigglin' and carrying on out there in his car; I hear you!

NURSE
*(Loud; to cover the sound of his voice)* I'm going, Father.

FATHER
All right; get along, then; get on!

NURSE
You're damned right!

FATHER
Go on! Go!
   *(The NURSE regards him for a moment; turns, exits)*
And don't stay out there all night in his car, when you get back. You hear me? *(Pause)* You hear me?
   *(Lights fade on this scene; come up on)*


SCENE THREE


A *bare area.* JACK *enters, addresses his remarks off*

*stage and to an invisible mirror on an invisible dresser.*
*Music under this scene, as though coming from a*
*distance.*

JACK

Hey . . . Bessie! C'mon, now. Hey . . . honey? Get your butt
out of bed . . . wake up. C'mon; the goddam afternoon's half
gone; we gotta get movin'. Hey . . . I called that son-of-a-
bitch in New York . . . *I* told him, all right. I told him what
you said. Wake up, baby, we gotta get out of this dump; I
gotta get you to Memphis 'fore seven o'clock . . . and then
. . . POW! . . . *we* are headin' straight north. Here we come;
NEW YORK. I told that bastard . . . I said: Look, you don't
have no exclusive rights on Bessie . . . nobody's got 'em . . .
Bessie is doin' you a favor . . . she's doin' you a goddam
favor. She don't *have* to sing for you. I said: Bessie's tired . . .
she don't wanna travel now. An' he said: You don't *wanna*
back out of this . . . Bessie told me *herself* . . . and I said:
Look . . . don't worry yourself . . . Bessie said she'd cut more
sides for you . . . she will . . . she'll make all the goddam new
records you want. . . . What I mean to say *is*, just don't you
get any ideas about havin' exclusive rights . . . because
nobody's got 'em. *(Giggles)* I told him you was free as a bird,
honey. Free as a goddam bird. *(Looks in at her, shakes his*
*head)* Some bird! I been downstairs to check us out. I go
downstairs to check us out, and I run into a friend of mine
. . . and we sit in the bar and have a few, and he says:
What're *you* doin' now; what're you doin' in this crummy
hotel? And I say: I am cartin' a bird around with me. I'm
cartin' her north; I got a fat lady upstairs; she is sleepin' off last
night. An' he says: You always got *some* fat lady upstairs,
somewhere; boy, I never seen it fail. An' I say: This ain't just
no plain fat lady I got upstairs . . . this is a celebrity, boy . . .
this is a rich old fat singin' lady . . . an' he laughed an' he

said: Boy, who you got up there? I say: You guess. An' he says: C'mon . . . I can't *guess*. An' I told him . . . I am travelin' with Miss Bessie Smith. An' he looked at me, an' he said, real quiet: Jesus, boy, are you travelin' with Bessie? An' I said . . . an' real proud: You're damn right I'm travelin' with Bessie. An' he wants to meet you; so you get your big self out of bed; we're goin' to go downstairs, 'cause I wanna show you off. C'mon, now; I mean I *gotta* show you off. 'Cause then he said: Whatever *happened* to Bessie? An' I said: What do you mean, whatever happened to Bessie? She's right upstairs. An' he said: I mean, what's she been doin' the past four-five years? There was a time there, boy, Chicago an' all, New York, she was the hottest goddam thing goin'. Is she still singin'? YOU HEAR THAT? That's what he said: Is she still singin'? An' I said . . . I said, you been tired . . . you been restin'. You ain't been forgotten, honey, but they are askin' questions. SO YOU GET UP! We're drivin' north tonight, an' when you get in New York . . . *you* show 'em where you been. Honey, you're gonna go back on top again . . . I mean it . . . you *are*. I'm gonna get you up to New York. 'Cause you gotta make that date. I mean, sure, baby, you're free as a goddam bird, an' I did tell that son-of-a-bitch he don't have exclusive rights on you . . . but, honey . . . he *is* interested . . . an' you gotta hustle for it now. You do; 'cause if you don't do *somethin'*, people are gonna stop askin' where you been the past four-five years . . . they're gonna stop askin' anything at all! You hear? An' if I say downstairs you're rich . . . that don't make it so, Bessie. No more, honey. You gotta make this goddam trip . . . you gotta get goin' again. *(Pleading)* Baby? Honey? You know I'm not lyin' to you. C'mon now; get up. We go downstairs to the bar an' have a few . . . see my friend . . . an' then we'll get in that car . . . and *go*. 'Cause it's gettin' late, honey . . . it's gettin' awful late. *(Brighter)* Hey! You awake? *(Moving to the wings)* Well, c'mon, then, Bessie . . . let's get up. We're goin' north again!

*(The lights fade on this scene.*
*Music.*
*The sunset is predominant)*

JACK'S VOICE
Ha, ha; thanks; thanks a lot. *(Car door slams. Car motor*
*starts)* O.K.; here we go; we're on our way. *(Sound of car*
*motor gunning, car moving off, fading)*
*(The sunset dims again.*
*Music, fading, as the lights come up on)*


SCENE FOUR

*The admissions room of the hospital. The* NURSE *is at*
*her desk; the* ORDERLY *stands to one side.*


ORDERLY
The mayor of Memphis! I went into his room and there he
was; the mayor of Memphis. Lying right there, flat on his
belly . . . a cigar in his mouth . . . an unlit cigar stuck in his
mouth, chewing on it, chewing on a big, unlit cigar . . .
shuffling a lot of papers in his hands, a pillow shoved up
under his chest to give him some freedom for all those papers
. . . and I came in, and I said: Good afternoon, Your Honor
. . . and he swung his face 'round and he looked at me and he
shouted: My ass hurts, you get the hell out of here!


NURSE *(Laughs freely)*
His Honor has got his ass in a sling, and that's for sure.


ORDERLY
And I got out; I left very quickly; I closed the door fast.

NURSE

The mayor and his hemorrhoids . . . the mayor's late hemorrhoids . . . are a matter of deep concern to this institution, for the mayor built this hospital; the mayor is here with his ass in a sling, and the seat of government is now in Room 206 . . . so you be nice and respectful. *(Laughs)* There is a man two rooms down who walked in here last night after you went off . . . that man walked in here with his hands over his gut to keep his insides from spilling right out on this desk . . .

ORDERLY

I heard. . . .

NURSE

. . . and that man may live, or he may not live, and the wagers are heavy that he will not live . . . but we are not one bit more concerned for that man than we are for His Honor . . . no sir.

ORDERLY *(Chuckling)*

I like your contempt.

NURSE

You what? You like my *contempt*, do you? Well now, don't misunderstand me. Just what do you think I meant? What have you got it in your mind that I was saying?

ORDERLY

Why, it's a matter of proportion. Surely you don't *condone* the fact that the mayor and his piles, and that poor man lying up there . . . ?

NURSE

*Condone!* Will you listen to that: condone! My! Aren't you the educated one? What . . . what does that word mean, boy? That word condone? Hunh? You do talk some, don't you? You have a great deal to learn. Now it's true that the poor man lying up there with his guts coming out could be a nigger for all the attention he'd get if His Honor should start shouting for something . . . he could be on the operating table . . . and they'd drop his insides right on the floor and come running if the mayor should want his cigar lit. . . . But that is the way things *are*. Those are facts. You had better acquaint yourself with some realities.

ORDERLY

I know . . . I know the mayor is an important man. He is impressive . . . even lying on his belly like he is. . . . I'd like to get to talk to him.

NURSE

Don't you know it! TALK to him! Talk to the mayor? What for?

ORDERLY

I've told you. I've told you I don't intend to stay here carrying crap pans and washing out the operating theatre until I have a . . . a long gray beard . . . I'm . . . I'm going beyond that.

NURSE *(Patronizing)*

Sure.

ORDERLY

*I've* told you . . . I'm going beyond that. This . . .

NURSE
*(Shakes her head in amused disbelief)* Oh, my. Listen . . . you should count yourself lucky, boy. Just what do you think is going to happen to you? Is His Honor, the mayor, going to rise up out of his sickbed and take a personal interest in you? Write a letter to the President, maybe? And is Mr. Roosevelt going to send his wife, Lady Eleanor, down here after you? Or is it in your plans that you are going to be handed a big fat scholarship somewhere to the north of Johns Hopkins? Boy, you just don't know! I'll tell you something . . . you are lucky as you are. Whatever do you expect?

ORDERLY
What's been promised. . . . Nothing more. Just that.

NURSE
Promised! Promised? Oh, boy, I'll tell you about promises. Don't you know yet that everything is promises . . . and that is all there is to it? Promises . . . nothing more! I am personally sick of promises. Would you like to hear a little poem? Would you like me to recite some verse for you? Here is a little poem: "You kiss the niggers and I'll kiss the Jews and we'll stay in the White House as long as we choose." And that . . . according to what I am told . . . that is what Mr. and Mrs. Roosevelt sit at the breakfast table and sing to each other over their orange juice, right in the White House. Promises, boy! Promises . . . and that is what they are going to stay.

ORDERLY
There are *some* people who believe in more than promises. . . .

NURSE
Hunh?

ORDERLY *(Cautious now)*

I say, there are some people who believe in more than promises; there are some people who believe in action.


NURSE

What's that? What did you say?


ORDERLY

Action . . . ac— . . . Never mind.


NURSE *(Her eyes narrow)*

No . . . no, go on now . . . action? What kind of action do you mean?


ORDERLY

I don't *mean* anything . . . all I said was . . .


NURSE

I heard you. You know . . . I know what you been doing. You been listening to the great white doctor again . . . that big, good-looking blond intern you *admire* so much because he is so liberal-thinking, eh? My suitor? *(Laughs)* My suitor . . . my very own white knight, who is wasting his time patching up decent folk right here when there is dying going on in Spain. *(Exaggerated)* Oh, there is dying in Spain. And he is held here! That's who you have been listening to.


ORDERLY

I don't mean that. . . . I don't pay any attention . . . *(Weakly)* to that kind of talk. I do my job here . . . I try to keep . . .

NURSE *(Contemptuous)*

You try to keep yourself on the good side of everybody, don't you, boy? You stand there and you nod your kinky little head and say yes'm, yes'm, at everything I say, and then when he's here you go off in a corner and you get him and you sympathize with him . . . you get him to tell you about . . . promises! . . . and . . . and . . . action! . . . I'll tell you right now, he's going to get himself into trouble . . . and you're helping him right along.

ORDERLY

No, now. I don't . . .

NURSE *(With some disgust)*

All that talk of his! Action! I know all what he talks about . . . like about that bunch of radicals came through here last spring . . . causing the rioting . . . that arson! Stuff like that. Didn't . . . didn't you have someone get banged up in that?

ORDERLY *(Contained)*

My uncle got run down by a lorry full of state police . . .

NURSE

. . . which the Governor called out because of the rioting . . . and that arson! Action! That was a fine bunch of action. Is that what you mean? Is that what you get him off in a corner and get him to talk about . . . and pretend you're interested? Listen, boy . . . if you're going to get yourself in with those folks, you'd better . . .

ORDERLY *(Quickly)*

I'm not mixed up with any folks . . . honestly . . . I'm not. I just want to . . .

NURSE

I'll tell you what you just want. . . . I'll tell you what you just
want if you have any mind to keep this good job you've
got. . . . You just shut your ears . . . and you keep that
mouth closed tight, too. All this talk about what you are going
to go beyond! You keep walking a real tight line here, and
. . . and at night . . . *(She begins to giggle)* . . . and at night,
if you want to, on your own time . . . at night you keep right
on putting that bleach on your hands and your neck and your
face . . .


ORDERLY

I do no such thing!


NURSE *(In full laughter)*
. . . and you keep right on bleaching away . . . b-l-e-a-c-h-
i-n-g a-w-a-y . . . but you do that on your own time . . . you
can do all that on your own time.


ORDERLY *(Pleading)*

I do no such thing!


NURSE

The hell you don't! You are such a . . .


ORDERLY

That kind of talk is very . . .


NURSE

. . . you are so mixed up! You are going to be one funny
sight. You, over there in a corner playing up to him . . . well,
boy, you are going to be one funny sight come the millen-
nium. . . . The great black mob marching down the street,

banners in the air . . . that great black mob . . . and you right there in the middle, your bleached-out, snowy-white face in the middle of the pack like that . . . *(She breaks down in laughter)* . . . oh . . . oh, my . . . oh. I tell you, that will be quite a sight.

                    ORDERLY *(Plaintive)*
I wish you'd stop that.

                    NURSE
Quite a sight.

                    ORDERLY
I wish you wouldn't make fun of me . . . I don't give you any cause.

                    NURSE
Oh, my . . . oh, I *am* sorry . . . I am *so* sorry.

                    ORDERLY
I don't think I give you any cause. . . .

                    NURSE
You don't, eh?

                    ORDERLY
No.

                    NURSE
Well . . . you *are* a true little gentleman, that's for sure . . . you *are* polite . . . and deferential . . . and you are a genuine little ass-licker, if I ever saw one. Tell me, boy . . .

ORDERLY

(Stiffening a little) There is no need . . .


NURSE

(Maliciously solicitous) Tell me, boy . . . is it true that you
have Uncle Tom'd yourself right out of the bosom of your
family . . . right out of your circle of acquaintances? Is it true,
young man, that you are now an inhabitant of no-man's-land,
on the one side shunned and disowned by your brethren, and
on the other an object of contempt and derision to your
betters? Is that your problem, son?


ORDERLY

You . . . you shouldn't do that. I . . . work hard . . . I try to
advance myself . . . I give nobody trouble.


NURSE

I'll tell you what you do. . . . You go north, boy . . . you go
up to New York City, where nobody's any better than
anybody else . . . get up north, boy. (Abrupt change of tone)
But before you do anything like that, you run on downstairs
and get me a pack of cigarettes.


ORDERLY

(Pauses. Is about to speak; thinks better of it; moves off to door,
rear) Yes'm.
            (Exits)


NURSE

(Watches him leave. After he is gone, shakes her head,
laughs, parodies him)
Yes'm . . . yes'm . . . ha, ha, ha! You white niggers kill me.
(She picks up her desk phone, dials a number, as the
lights come up on)

## SCENE FIVE

*Which is both the hospital set of the preceding scene*
*and, as well, on the raised platform, another admis-*
*sions desk of another hospital. The desk is empty. The*
*phone rings, twice. The* SECOND NURSE *comes in,*
*slowly, filing her nails, maybe.*

SECOND NURSE
*(Lazily answering the phone)* Mercy Hospital.

NURSE
Mercy Hospital! Mercy, indeed, you away from your desk all
the time. *Some* hospitals are run better than *others; some*
nurses stay at their posts.

SECOND NURSE *(Bored)*
Oh, hi. What do you want?

NURSE
I don't *want* anything. . . .

SECOND NURSE
*(Pause)* Oh. Well, what did you call for?

NURSE
I didn't call *for* anything. I *(Shrugs)* just called.

SECOND NURSE
Oh.
*(The lights dim a little on the two nurses.*
*Music.*
*Car sounds up)*

JACK'S VOICE

(*Laughs*) I tell you, honey, he didn't like that. No, sir, he didn't. You comfortable, honey. Hunh? You just lean back and enjoy the ride, baby; we're makin' good time. Yes, we are makin' . . . WATCH OUT! WATCH . . .

(*Sound of crash. . . . Silence*)

Honey . . . baby . . . we have crashed . . . you all right? . . . BESSIE! BESSIE!

(*Music up again, fading as the lights come up full again on the two nurses*)


NURSE

. . . and, what else? Oh, yeah; *we* have got the mayor here.


SECOND NURSE

That's nice. What's he doin'?


NURSE

He isn't *doin'* anything; he is a patient here.


SECOND NURSE

Oh. Well, *we* had the mayor's wife *here* . . . last April.


·NURSE

Unh-hunh. Well, *we* got the mayor *here*, now.


SECOND NURSE (*Very bored*)

Unh-hunh. Well, that's nice.


NURSE

(*Turns, sees the* INTERN *entering*) Oh, lover-boy just walked in; I'll call you later, hunh?

SECOND NURSE

Unh-hunh.

>(*They both hang up. The lights fade on the* SECOND
NURSE)

## SCENE SIX

NURSE

Well, how is the Great White Doctor this evening?

INTERN (*Irritable*)

Oh . . . drop it.

NURSE

Oh, my . . . where is your cheerful demeanor this evening,
Doctor?

INTERN

(*Smiling in spite of himself*) How do you do it? How do you
manage to just dismiss things from your mind? How can you
say a . . . cheerful hello to someone . . . dismissing from
your mind . . . excusing yourself for the vile things you have
said the evening before?

NURSE (*Lightly*)

I said nothing vile. I put you in your place . . . that's all. I
. . . I merely put you in your place . . . as I have done before
. . . and as I shall do again.

INTERN

*(Is about to say something; thinks better of it; sighs)* Never
mind . . . forget about it . . . Did you *see* the sunset?

NURSE *(Mimicking)*

No, I didn't *see* the sunset. *What* is it doing?

INTERN

*(Amused. Puts it on heavily)* The west is burning . . . fire has
enveloped fully half of the continent . . . the . . . the fingers
of the flame stretch upward to the stars . . . and . . . and
there is a monstrous burning circumference hanging on the
edge of the world.

NURSE *(Laughs)*

Oh, my . . . oh, my.

INTERN *(Serious)*

It's a truly beautiful sight. Go out and have a look.

NURSE *(Coquettish)*

Oh, Doctor, I am chained to my desk of pain, so I must rely
on you. . . . Talk the sunset to me, you . . . you monstrous
burning intern hanging on the edge of my circumference . . .
ha, ha, *ha*.

INTERN

*(Leans toward her)* When?

NURSE

When?

INTERN *(Lightly)*
When . . . when are you going to let me nearer, woman?


NURSE
Oh, my!


INTERN
Here am I . . . here am I tangential, while all the while I
would serve more nobly as a radiant, not outward from, but
reversed, plunging straight to your lovely vortex.


NURSE *(Laughs)*
Oh, la! You must keep your mind off my lovely vortex . . .
you just remain . . . uh . . . tangential.


INTERN *(Mock despair)*
*How* is a man to fulfill himself? Here I offer you love . . .
consider the word . . . love. . . . Here I offer you my love,
my self . . . my bored bed . . .


NURSE
I note your offer . . . your offer is noted. *(Holds out a clip
board)* Here . . . do you want your reports?


INTERN
No . . . I don't want my reports. Give them here. *(Takes the
clip board)*


NURSE
And while you're here with your hot breath on me, hand me
a cigarette. I sent the nigger down for a pack. I ran out. *(He
gives her a cigarette)* Match?

INTERN

Go light it on the sunset. *(Tosses match to her)* He says you owe him for three packs.


NURSE

*(Lights her cigarette)* Your bored bed . . . indeed.


INTERN

Ma'am . . . the heart yearns, the body burns . . .


NURSE

And *I* haven't time for *in*terns.


INTERN

. . . the heart yearns, the body burns . . . and I haven't time . . . Oh, I don't know . . . the things you women can do to art.
   *(More intimate, but still light)*
Have you told your father, yet? Have you told your father that I am hopelessly in love with you? Have you told him that at night the sheets of my bed are like a tent, poled center-upward in my love for you?


NURSE *(Wry)*

I'll tell him . . . I'll tell my father just that . . . just what you said . . . and he'll be down here after you for talking to a young lady like that! Really!


INTERN

My God! I forgot myself! A cloistered maiden in whose house trousers are never mentioned . . . in which flies, I am sure, are referred to only as winged bugs. Here I thought I was talking to someone, to a certain young nurse, whose collection of anatomical jokes for all occasions . . .


NURSE *(Giggles)*

Oh, you be still, now. *(Lofty)* Besides, just because I play coarse and flip around here . . . to keep my place with the rest of you . . . don't you think for a minute that I relish this turn to the particular from the general. . . . If you don't mind, we'll just cease this talk.


INTERN *(Half sung)*

I'm always in tumescence for you. You'd never guess the things I . . .


NURSE *(Blush-giggle)*

Now stop that! Really, I mean it!


INTERN

Then marry me, woman. If nothing else, marry me.


NURSE

Don't, now.


INTERN

*(Joking and serious at the same time)* Marry me.


NURSE

*(Matter-of-fact, but not unkindly)* I am sick of this talk. My poor father may have some funny ideas; he may be having a pretty hard time reconciling himself to things as they are. But not me! Forty-six dollars a month! Isn't that right? Isn't that what you make? Forty-six dollars a month! Boy, you can't

afford even to think about marrying. You can't afford marriage. . . . Best you can afford is lust. That's the best you can afford.

NURSE

INTERN *(Scathing)*
Oh . . . gentle woman . . . nineteenth-century lady out of place in this vulgar time . . . maiden versed in petit point and murmured talk of the weather . . .

NURSE
Now I mean it . . . you can cut that talk right out.

INTERN
. . . type my great-grandfather fought and died for . . . forty-six dollars a month and the best I can afford is lust! Jesus, woman!

NURSE
All right . . . you can quit making fun of me. You can quit it right this minute.

INTERN
*I!* Making fun of *you* . . . !

NURSE
I am tired of being toyed with; I am tired of your impractical propositions. Must you dwell on what is not going to happen? Must you ask me, constantly, over and over again, the same question to which you are already aware you will get the same answer? Do you get pleasure from it? What unreasonable form of contentment do you derive from persisting in this?

INTERN *(Lightly)*
Because I love you?


NURSE
Oh, that would help matters along; it really would . . . even if
it were *true*. The economic realities would pick up their skirts,
whoop, and depart before the lance-high, love-smit knight.
My knight, whose real and true interest, if we come right
down to it, as indicated in the order of your propositions, is,
and always has been, a convenient and uncomplicated
bedding down.


INTERN
*(Smiling, and with great gallantry)* I have offered to marry
you.


NURSE
Yeah . . . sure . . . you have offered to marry me. The
United States is chuck-full of girls who have heard that great
promise—I will marry you . . . I will marry you . . . IF! If!
The great promise with its great conditional attached to
it. . . .


INTERN *(Amused)*
Who are you pretending to be?


NURSE *(Abrupt)*
What do you mean?


INTERN *(Laughing)*
Oh, *nothing*.

NURSE

*(Regards him silently for a moment; then)* Marry me! Do you know . . . do you know that nigger I sent to fetch me a pack of butts . . . do you know he is in a far better position . . . realistically, economically . . . to ask to marry me than you are? Hunh? Do you know that? That nigger! Do you know that nigger outearns you . . . and by a *lot?*

INTERN

*(Bows to her)* I know he does . . . and I know what value you, you and your famous family, put on such things. So, I have an idea for you . . . why don't you just *ask* that nigger to marry you? 'Cause, boy, he'd never ask you! I'm sure if you told your father about it, it would give him some pause at first, because we know what type of man your father is . . . don't we? . . . But then he would think about it . . . and realize the advantages of the match . . . realistically . . . economically . . . and he would find some way to adjust his values, in consideration of your happiness, and security. . . .

NURSE

*(Flicks her still-lit cigarette at him, hard; hits him with it)* You are disgusting!

INTERN

Damn you, bitch!

NURSE

Disgusting!

INTERN

Realistic . . . practical . . . *(A little softer, now)* Your family is a famous *name,* but those thousand acres are *gone,* and the

pillars of your house are blistered and flaking . . . *(Harder)*
Not that your family ever *had*, within human memory, a
thousand acres to *go* . . . *or* a house with pillars in the first
place. . . .

NURSE *(Angry)*
I am fully aware of what is true and what is not true. *(Soberly)*
Go about your work and leave me be.

INTERN *(Sweetly)*
Aw.

NURSE
I said . . . leave me be.

INTERN
*(Brushing himself)* It is a criminal offense to set fire to interns
. . . orderlies you may burn at will, unless you have other
plans for them . . . but interns . . .

NURSE
. . . are a dime a dozen. *(Giggles)* Did I burn you?

INTERN
No, you did not burn me.

NURSE
That's too bad . . . would have served you right if I had.
*(Pauses; then smiles)* I'm sorry, honey.

INTERN *(Mock formal)*
I accept your apology . . . and I await your surrender.

NURSE *(Laughs)*
Well, you just await it. *(A pause)* Hey, what are you going to
do about the mayor being here now?


INTERN
What am I supposed to do about it? I am on emergencies, and
he is not an emergency case.


NURSE
I told you . . . I told you what you should do.


INTERN
I know . . . I should go upstairs to his room . . . I should pull
up a chair, and I should sit down and I should say, How's
tricks, Your Honor?


NURSE
Well, you make fun if you want to . . . but if you listen to
me, you'll know you need some people *behind* you.


INTERN
Strangers!


NURSE
Strangers don't stay strangers . . . not if you don't let them.
He could do something for you if he had a mind to.


INTERN
Yes he could . . . indeed, he *could* do something for me. . . .
He could give me his car . . . he could make me a present of
his Cord automobile. . . . That would be the finest thing any
mayor ever did for a private citizen. Have you seen that car?

NURSE

Have I seen that car? Have I seen this . . . have I seen that?
Cord automobiles and . . . and sunsets . . . those are . . .
fine preoccupations. Is that what you think about? Huh?
Driving a fine car into a fine sunset?


INTERN *(Quietly)*

Lord knows, I'd like to get away from here.


NURSE *(Nodding)*

I know . . . I know. Well, maybe you're going to *have* to get
away from here. People are aware how dissatisfied you are
. . . people have heard a lot about your . . . dissatisfactions. . . . My father has heard . . . people got wind of the
way you feel about things. People here aren't good enough for
your attentions. . . . Foreigners . . . a bunch of foreigners
who are cutting each other up in their own business . . .
that's where you'd like to be, isn't it?


INTERN *(Quietly; intensely)*

There are over half a million people killed in that war! Do you
know that? By airplanes. . . . Civilians! You misunderstand
me so! I am . . . all right . . . this way. . . . My dissatisfactions . . . you call them that . . . my dissatisfactions have
nothing to do with loyalties. . . . I am not concerned with
politics . . . but I have a sense of urgency . . . a dislike of
waste . . . stagnation . . . I am *stranded . . . here*. . . . My
talents are not large . . . but the emergencies of the emergency ward of this second-rate hospital in this second-rate
state . . . No! . . . it isn't enough. Oh, you listen to me. If I
could . . . if I could bandage the arm of one person . . . if I
could be over there right this minute . . . you could take the
city of Memphis . . . you could take the whole state . . . and

don't you forget I was born here . . . you could take the whole goddam state. . . .

NURSE *(Hard)*
Well, I have a very good idea of how we could arrange that. I have a dandy idea. . . . We could just tell the mayor about the way you feel, and he'd be delighted to help you on your way . . . out of this hospital at the very least, and maybe out of the state! And I don't think he'd be giving you any Cord automobile as a going-away present, either. He'd set you out, all right . . . he'd set you right out on your *butt!* That's what he'd do.

INTERN
*(With a rueful half-smile)* Yes . . . yes . . . I imagine he would. I feel lucky . . . I feel doubly fortunate, now . . . having you . . . feeling the way we do about each other.

NURSE
You are so sarcastic!

INTERN
Well, how the hell do you expect me to behave?

NURSE
Just . . . *(Laughs)* . . . oh, boy, this is good . . . just like I told the nigger . . . you walk a straight line, and you do your job . . . *(Turns coy, here)* . . . and . . . and unless you are kept late by some emergency more pressing than your . . . *(Smiles wryly)* . . . "love" . . . for me . . . I may let you drive me home tonight . . . in your beat-up Chevy.

INTERN

Woman, as always I anticipate with enormous pleasure the prospect of driving you home . . . a stop along the way . . . fifteen minutes or so . . . of tantalizing preliminary love play ending in an infuriating and inconclusive wrestling match, during which you hiss of the . . . the liberties I should not take, and I sound the horn once or twice accidentally with my elbow . . .

(*She giggles at this*)

. . . and finally, in my beat-up car, in front of your father's beat-up house . . . a kiss of searing intensity . . . a hand in the right place . . . briefly . . . and your hasty departure within. I am looking forward to this ritual . . . as I always do.

NURSE *(Pleased)*

Why, thank you.


INTERN

I look forward to this ritual because of how it sets me apart from other men . . .


NURSE

Aw . . .


INTERN

. . . because I am probably the only white man under sixty in two counties who has *not* had the pleasure of . . .


NURSE

LIAR! You no-account mother-grabbing son of a nigger!


INTERN *(Laughs)*

Boy! Watch you go!

NURSE

FILTH! You are filth!


INTERN

I am honest . . . an honest man. Let me make you an honest
woman.


NURSE

(Steaming . . . her rage between her teeth) You have done it,
boy . . . you have played around with me and you have done
it. I am going to get you . . . I am going to fix you . . . I am
going to see to it that you are *through* here . . . do you
understand what I'm telling you?


INTERN

There is no ambiguity in your talk now, honey.


NURSE

You're damn right there isn't.
          (The ORDERLY *re-enters from stage-rear. The* NURSE
          *sees him*)
Get out of here!
          (But *he stands there*)
Do you hear me? You get the hell out of here! GO!
          (He *retreats, exits, to silence*)


INTERN (Chuckling)

King of the castle. My, you *are* something.


NURSE

Did you get what I was telling you?

INTERN
Why, I heard every word . . . every sweet syllable. . . .


NURSE
You have overstepped yourself . . . and you are going to wish
you hadn't. I'll get my father . . . I'll have you done with
*myself.*


INTERN *(Cautious)*
Aw, come on, now.


NURSE
I mean it.


INTERN *(Lying badly)*
Now look . . . you don't think I meant . . .


NURSE *(Mimicking)*
Now you don't think I meant . . . *(Laughs broadly)* Oh, my
. . . you are the funny one.
     *(Her threat, now, has no fury, but is filled with quiet
     conviction)*
I said I'll fix you . . . and I will. You just go along with your
work . . . you do your job . . . but what I said . . . you keep
that burning in the back of your brain. We'll go right along,
you and I, and we'll be civil . . . and it'll be as though
nothing had happened . . . nothing at all. *(Laughs again)*
Honey, your neck is in the *noose* . . . and I have a whip . . .
and I'll set the horse from under you . . . when it pleases me.


INTERN *(Wryly)*
It's going to be nice around here.

NURSE

Oh, yes it is. I'm going to enjoy it . . . I really am.


INTERN

Well . . . I'll forget about driving you home tonight. . . .


NURSE

Oh, no . . . you will *not* forget about driving me home tonight. You will drive me home *tonight* . . . you will drive me home *tonight* . . . and *tomorrow* night . . . you will see me to my *door* . . . you will be my gallant. We will have things between us a little bit the way I am told things *used* to be. You will *court* me, boy, and you will do it *right!*


INTERN

*(Stares at her for a moment)* You impress me. No matter what else, I've got to admit that.
        *(The* NURSE *laughs wildly at this.*
        *Music.*
        *The lights on this hospital set fade, and come up on the* SECOND NURSE, *at her desk, for)*


## SCENE SEVEN


JACK

*(Rushing in)* Ma'am, I need help, quick!


SECOND NURSE

What d'you want here?

JACK

There has been an accident, ma'am . . . I got an injured
woman outside in my car. . . .


SECOND NURSE

Yeah? Is that so? Well, you sit down and wait. . . . You go
over there and sit down and wait a while.


JACK

This is an emergency! There has been an accident!


SECOND NURSE

YOU WAIT! You just sit down and wait!


JACK

This woman is badly hurt. . . .


SECOND NURSE

YOU COOL YOUR HEELS!


JACK

Ma'am . . . I got Bessie Smith out in that car there. . . .


SECOND NURSE

I DON'T CARE WHO YOU GOT OUT THERE,
NIGGER. YOU COOL YOUR HEELS!
(*Music up.*
*The lights fade on this scene, come up again on the*
*main hospital scene, on the* NURSE *and the* INTERN,
*for*)

## SCENE EIGHT

*(Music fades)*

NURSE *(Loud)*
Hey, nigger . . . nigger!
*(The* ORDERLY *re-enters)*
Give me my cigarettes.

INTERN
I think I'll . . .

NURSE
You stay here!
*(The* ORDERLY *hands the* NURSE *the cigarettes,
cautious and attentive to see what is wrong)*
A person could die for a smoke, the time you take. What'd
you do . . . sit downstairs in the can and rest your small,
shapely feet . . . hunh?

ORDERLY
You told me to . . . go back outside . . .

NURSE
Before that! What'd you do . . . go to the cigarette *factory?*
Did you take a quick run up to Winston-Salem for these?

ORDERLY
No . . . I . . .

NURSE
Skip it. *(To the* INTERN*)* Where? Where were you planning to
go?

INTERN *(Too formal)*

I beg your pardon?

NURSE

I said . . . where did you want to go to? Were you off for coffee?

INTERN

Is that what you want? Now that you have your cigarettes, have you hit upon the idea of having coffee, too? Now that he is back from one errand, are you planning to send me on another?

NURSE *(Smiling wickedly)*

Yeah . . . I think I'd like that . . . keep both of you jumping. I *would* like coffee, and I *would* like you to get it for me. So why don't you just trot right across the hall and get me some? And I like it good and hot . . . and strong . . .

INTERN

. . . and black . . . ?

NURSE

Cream! . . . and sweet . . . and in a hurry!

INTERN

I guess your wish is my command . . . hunh?

NURSE

You bet it is!

INTERN
*(Moves halfway to the door, stage-rear, then pauses)*
I just had a lovely thought . . . that maybe sometime when
you are sitting there at your desk opening mail with that
stiletto you use for a letter opener, you might slip and tear
open your arm . . . then you could come running into the
emergency . . . and I could be there when you came running
in, blood coming out of you like water out of a faucet . . . and
I could take ahold of your arm . . . and just hold it . . . just
hold it . . . and watch it flow . . . just hold on to you and
watch your blood flow. . . .


NURSE
*(Grabs up the letter opener . . . holds it up)*
This? More likely between your ribs!


INTERN *(Exiting)*
One coffee, lady.


NURSE
*(After a moment of silence, throws the letter opener
back down on her desk)*
I'll take care of him. CRACK! I'll crack that whip. *(To the*
ORDERLY) What are you standing there for . . . hunh? You
like to watch what's going on?


ORDERLY
I'm no voyeur.


NURSE
You what? You like to listen in? You take pleasure in it?

ORDERLY

I said no.


NURSE *(Half to herself)*
I'll bet you don't. I'll take care of him . . . talking to me like
that . . . I'll crack that whip. Let him just wait.
*(To the* ORDERLY, *now)*
My father says that Francisco Franco is going to be victorious
in that war over there . . . that he's going to win . . . and that
it's just wonderful.


ORDERLY

He does?


NURSE
Yes, he does. My father says that Francisco Franco has got
them licked, and that they're a bunch of radicals, anyway,
and it's all to the good . . . just wonderful.


ORDERLY

Is that so?


NURSE
I've told you my father is a . . . a historian, so he isn't just
anybody. His opinion counts for something special. It *still*
counts for something special. He says anybody wants to go
over there and get mixed up in that thing has got it coming to
him . . . whatever happens.


ORDERLY
I'm sure your father is an informed man, and . . .

NURSE

What?


ORDERLY

I said . . . I said . . . I'm sure your father is an informed man,
and . . . his opinion is to be respected.


NURSE

That's right, boy . . . you just jump to it and say what you
think people want to hear . . . you be both sides of the coin.
Did you . . . did you hear him threaten me there? Did you?


ORDERLY

Oh, now . . . I don't think . . .


NURSE *(Steely)*

You heard him threaten me!


ORDERLY

I don't think . . .


NURSE

For such a smart boy . . . you are so dumb. I don't know what
I am going to do with you.
     *(She is thinking of the* INTERN *now, and her expres-
     sion shows it)*
You refuse to comprehend things and that bodes badly . . . it
does. Especially considering it is all but arranged . . .


ORDERLY

What is all but arranged?

NURSE

*(A great laugh, but mirthless. She is barely under control)*

Why, don't you know, boy? Didn't you know that you and I are practically engaged?

ORDERLY

I . . . I don't . . .

NURSE

Don't you know about the economic realities? Haven't you been appraised of the way things *are?* *(She giggles)* Our knights are gone forth into sunsets . . . behind the wheels of Cord cars . . . the acres have diminished and the paint is flaking . . . that there is a great . . . *abandonment?*

ORDERLY *(Cautious)*

I don't understand you. . . .

NURSE

No kidding? *(Her voice shakes)* No kidding . . . you don't understand me? Why? What's the matter, boy, don't you get the idea?

ORDERLY *(Contained, but angry)*

I think you'd tire of riding me some day. I think you *would.* . . .

NURSE

You go up to Room 206, right now . . . you go up and tell the mayor that when his butt's better we have a marrying job for him.

ORDERLY (With some distaste)
Really . . . you go much too far. . . .


NURSE

Oh, I do, do I? Well, let me tell you something . . . I am sick
of it! I am *sick*. I am sick of everything in this hot, stupid, fly-
ridden *world*. I am sick of the disparity between things as they
are, and as they should be! I am sick of this desk . . . this
uniform . . . it scratches. . . . I am sick of the sight of *you*
. . . the *thought* of you makes me . . . *itch*. . . . I am sick of
*him*. (*Soft now: a chant*) I am sick of talking to people on the
phone in this damn stupid hospital. . . . I am sick of the
smell of Lysol . . . I could die of it. . . . I am sick of going to
bed and I am sick of waking up. . . . I am tired . . . I am tired
of the truth . . . and I am tired of lying about the truth . . . I
am tired of my skin. . . . I WANT OUT!


ORDERLY

(*After a short pause*) Why don't you go into emergency . . .
and lie down?
(*He approaches her*)


NURSE

Keep away from me.
(*At this moment the outside door bursts open and*
JACK *plunges into the room. He is all these things:*
*drunk, shocked, frightened. His face should be cut,*
*but no longer bleeding. His clothes should be dirtied*
*. . . and in some disarray. He pauses, a few steps into*
*the room, breathing hard*)


NURSE

Whoa! Hold on there, you.

ORDERLY *(Not advancing)*
What do you want?


JACK
*(After more hard breathing; confused)* What . . . ?


NURSE
You come banging in through that door like that? What's the
matter with you? *(To the* ORDERLY*)* Go see what's the matter
with him.


ORDERLY *(Advancing slightly)*
What do you *want?*


JACK *(Very confused)*
What do I want . . . ?


ORDERLY *(Backing off)*
You can't come in here like this . . . banging your way in
here . . . don't you know any better?


NURSE
You drunk?


JACK
*(Taken aback by the irrelevance)* I've been drinking . . . yes
. . . all right . . . I'm drunk. *(Intense)* I got someone outside . . .


NURSE
You stop that yelling. This is a white hospital, you.

ORDERLY *(Nearer the* NURSE*)*
That's right. She's right. This is a private hospital . . . a
semiprivate hospital. If you go on . . . into the city . . .

JACK *(Shakes his head)*
No. . . .

NURSE
Now you listen to me, and you get this straight . . .
*(Pauses just perceptibly, then says the word, but with no
special emphasis)* . . . nigger . . . this is a semiprivate white
hospital . . .

JACK *(Defiant)*
I don't care!

NURSE
Well, you *get* on. . . .

ORDERLY
*(As the* INTERN *re-enters with two containers of coffee)*
You go on now . . . you go . . .

INTERN
What's all this about?

ORDERLY
I told him to go on into Memphis . . .

INTERN
Be quiet. *(To* JACK*)* What is all this about?

JACK

Please . . . I got a woman . . .


NURSE

You been told to move on.


INTERN

You got a woman . . .


JACK

Outside . . . in the car. . . . There was an accident . . . there
is blood. . . . Her arm . . .


INTERN
*(After thinking for a moment, looking at the* NURSE,
*moves toward the outside door)*
All right . . . we'll go see. *(To the* ORDERLY, *who hangs back)*
Come on, you . . . let's go.


ORDERLY
*(Looks to the* NURSE*)* We told him to go on into Memphis.


NURSE
*(To the* INTERN, *her eyes narrowing)* Don't you go out there!


INTERN
*(Ignoring her; to the* ORDERLY*)* You heard me . . . come on!


NURSE *(Strong)*
I told you . . . DON'T GO OUT THERE!

INTERN *(Softly, sadly)*
Honey . . . you going to fix me? You going to have the mayor throw me out of here on my butt? Or are you going to arrange it in Washington to have me *deported?* What *are* you going to do . . . hunh?

NURSE *(Between her teeth)*
Don't go out there. . . .

INTERN
Well, honey, whatever it is you're going to do . . . it might as well be now as any other time.
*(He and the* ORDERLY *move to the outside door)*

NURSE
*(Half angry, half plaintive, as they exit)*
Don't go!
*(After they exit)*
I warn you! I *will* fix you. You go out that door . . . you're through here.
*(*JACK *moves to a vacant area near the bench, stage-right. The* NURSE *lights a cigarette)*
I told you I'd fix you . . . I'll fix you. *(Now, to* JACK*)* I think I said this was a white hospital.

JACK *(Wearily)*
I know, lady . . . you told me.

NURSE
*(Her attention on the door)* You don't have sense enough to do what you're told . . . you make trouble for yourself . . . you make trouble for other people.

JACK *(Sighing)*

I don't care. . . .

NURSE

You'll care!

JACK

*(Softly, shaking his head)* No . . . I won't care. *(Now, half to her, half to himself)* We were driving along . . . not very fast . . . I don't think we were driving fast . . . we were in a hurry, yes . . . and I had been drinking . . . *we* had been drinking . . . but I *don't* think we were driving fast . . . not too fast . . .

NURSE
*(Her speeches now are soft comments on his)*
. . . driving drunk on the road . . . it not even dark yet . . .

JACK
. . . but then there was a car . . . I hadn't seen it . . . it couldn't have seen me . . . from a side road . . . hard, fast, sudden . . . *(Stiffens)* . . . CRASH! *(Loosens)* . . . and we weren't thrown . . . both of us . . . both cars stayed on the road . . . but we were stopped . . . my motor, running. . . . I turned it off . . . the door . . . the right door was all smashed in. . . . That's all it was . . . no more damage than that . . . but we had been riding along . . . laughing . . . it was cool driving, but it was warm out . . . and she had her arm out the window . . .

NURSE
. . . serves you right . . . drinking on the road . . .

JACK

. . . and I said . . . I said, Honey, we have crashed . . . you all right? *(His face contorts)* And I looked . . . and the door was all pushed in . . . she was caught there . . . where the door had pushed in . . . her right side, crushed into the torn door, the door crushed into her right side. . . . BESSIE! BESSIE! . . . *(More to the* NURSE, *now)* . . . but ma'am . . . her arm . . . her right arm . . . was torn off . . . almost torn off from her shoulder . . . and there was blood . . . SHE WAS BLEEDING SO . . . !

NURSE *(From a distance)*

Like water from a faucet . . . ? Oh, that is terrible . . . terrible. . . .

JACK

I didn't wait for nothin' . . . the other people . . . the other car . . . I started up . . . I started . . .

NURSE *(More alert)*

You took *off*? . . . You took off from an accident?

JACK

Her arm, ma'am . . .

NURSE

You probably got police looking for you right now . . . you know that?

JACK

Yes, ma'am . . . I suppose so . . . and I drove . . . there was a hospital about a mile up . . .

NURSE
*(Snapping to attention)* THERE! You went somewhere *else?*
You been somewhere else already? What are you doing *here*
with that woman then, hunh?

JACK
At the hospital . . . I came in to the desk and I told them what
had happened . . . and they said, you sit down and wait . . .
you go over there and sit down and wait a while. WAIT! It
was a white hospital, ma'am . . .

NURSE
*This* is a white hospital, too.

JACK
I said . . . this is an emergency . . . there has been an
accident. . . . YOU WAIT! You just sit down and wait. . . .
I told them . . . I told them it was an emergency . . . I said
. . . this woman is badly hurt. . . . YOU COOL YOUR
HEELS! . . . I said, Ma'am, I got Bessie Smith out in that car
there. . . . I DON'T CARE WHO YOU GOT OUT
THERE, NIGGER . . . YOU COOL YOUR HEELS! . . . I
couldn't wait there . . . her in the car . . . so I left there . . . I
drove on . . . I stopped on the road and I was told where to
come . . . and I came here.

NURSE *(Numb, distant)*
I know who she is . . . I heard her sing. *(Abruptly)* You give
me your name! You can't take off from an accident like that
. . . I'll phone the police; I'll tell them where you are!
> *(The* INTERN *and the* ORDERLY *re-enter. Their uni-*
> *forms are bloodied. The* ORDERLY *moves stage-rear,*
> *avoiding* JACK. *The* INTERN *moves in, staring at* JACK*)*

NURSE

He drove away from an accident . . . he just took off . . . and he didn't come right here, either . . . he's been to one hospital *already*. I *warned* you not to get mixed up in this. . . .

INTERN *(Softly)*

Shut up!
    *(Moves toward* JACK, *stops in front of him)*
You tell me something . . .

NURSE

I warned you! You didn't listen to me . . .

JACK

You want my name, too . . . is that what you want?

INTERN

No, that's not what I want.
    *(He is contained, but there is a violent emotion inside him)*
You tell me something. When you brought her here . . .

JACK

I brought her here . . . They wouldn't help her. . . .

INTERN

All right. When you brought her here . . . when you brought this woman *here* . . .

NURSE

Oh, this is no plain woman . . . this is no ordinary nigger . . . this is Bessie Smith!

INTERN

When you brought this woman *here* . . . when you drove up
*here* . . . when you brought this woman *here* . . . DID YOU
KNOW SHE WAS DEAD?
(*Pause*)


NURSE

Dead! . . . This nigger brought a dead woman here?


INTERN

(*Afraid of the answer*) Well . . . ?


NURSE (*Distantly*)

Dead . . . dead.


JACK

(*Wearily; turning, moving toward the outside door*) Yes . . . I
knew she was dead. She died on the way here.


NURSE

(*Snapping to*) Where you going? Where do you think you're
going? I'm going to get the police here for you!


JACK

(*At the door*)
Just outside.


INTERN

(*As* JACK *exits*)
WHAT DID YOU EXPECT ME TO DO, EH? WHAT
WAS I SUPPOSED TO DO?
(JACK *pauses for a moment, looks at him blankly,
closes the door behind him*)

TELL ME! WHAT WAS I SUPPOSED TO DO?

NURSE *(Slyly)*

Maybe . . . maybe he thought you'd bring her back to life
. . . great white doctor. *(Her laughter begins now, mounts to
hysteria)* Great . . . white . . . doctor. . . . Where are you
going to go now . . . great . . . white . . . doctor? You are
finished. You have had your last patient here. . . . Off you
go, boy! You have had your last patient . . . a nigger . . . a
dead nigger lady . . . WHO SINGS. Well . . . I sing, too,
boy . . . I sing real good. You want to hear me sing? Hunh?
You want to hear the way I sing? HUNH?
> *(Here she begins to sing and laugh at the same time.
> The singing is tuneless, almost keening, and the
> laughter is almost crying)*

INTERN

> *(Moves to her)*

Stop that! Stop that!
> *(But she can't. Finally he slaps her hard across the
> face. Silence. She is frozen, with her hand to her face
> where he hit her. He backs toward the rear door)*

ORDERLY

> *(His back to the wall)*

I never heard of such a thing . . . bringing a dead woman
here like that. . . . I don't know what people can be thinking
of sometimes. . . .
> *(The INTERN exits. The room fades into silhouette
> again. . . . The great sunset blazes; music up)*

CURTAIN

# The Sandbox

A BRIEF PLAY, IN MEMORY OF MY
GRANDMOTHER (1876–1959)

FIRST PERFORMANCE
April 15, 1960, New York City.

The Jazz Gallery.


Music by William Flanagan

# THE PLAYERS

### THE YOUNG MAN

*25. A good-looking, well-built boy in a bathing suit.*

### MOMMY

*55. A well-dressed, imposing woman.*

### DADDY

*60. A small man; gray, thin.*

### GRANDMA

*86. A tiny, wizened woman with bright eyes.*

### THE MUSICIAN

*No particular age, but young would be nice.*

*Note:*

When, in the course of the play, MOMMY and DADDY call each other by these names, there should be no suggestion of regionalism. These names are of empty affection and point up the pre-senility and vacuity of their characters.

# THE SCENE

*A bare stage, with only the following: Near the footlights, far
stage-right, two simple chairs set side by side, facing the
audience; near the footlights, far stage-left, a chair facing
stage-right with a music stand before it; farther back, and
stage-center, slightly elevated and raked, a large child's
sandbox with a toy pail and shovel; the background is the sky,
which alters from brightest day to deepest night.*

*At the beginning, it is brightest day; the* YOUNG MAN *is
alone on stage, to the rear of the sandbox, and to one side. He
is doing calisthenics; he does calisthenics until quite at the very
end of the play. These calisthenics, employing the arms only,
should suggest the beating and fluttering of wings. The*
YOUNG MAN *is, after all, the Angel of Death.*

MOMMY *and* DADDY *enter from stage-left,* MOMMY *first.*

MOMMY
*(Motioning to* DADDY*)* Well, here we are; this is the beach.

DADDY *(Whining)*
I'm cold.

MOMMY
*(Dismissing him with a little laugh)* Don't be silly; it's as warm as toast. Look at that nice young man over there: *he* doesn't think it's cold. *(Waves to the* YOUNG MAN*)* Hello.

YOUNG MAN
*(With an endearing smile)* Hi!

MOMMY *(Looking about)*
This will do perfectly . . . don't you think so, Daddy? There's sand there . . . and the water beyond. What do you think, Daddy?

DADDY *(Vaguely)*
Whatever you say, Mommy.

MOMMY
*(With the same little laugh)* Well, of course . . . whatever I say. Then, it's settled, is it?

DADDY *(Shrugs)*
She's *your* mother, not mine.


MOMMY
I know she's my mother. What do you take me for? *(A pause)*
All right, now; let's get on with it. *(She shouts into the wings,
stage-left)* You! Out there! You can come in now.
   *(The* MUSICIAN *enters, seats himself in the chair,
   stage-left, places music on the music stand, is ready to
   play.* MOMMY *nods approvingly)*


MOMMY
Very nice; very nice. Are you ready, Daddy? Let's go get
Grandma.


DADDY
Whatever you say, Mommy.


MOMMY
*(Leading the way out, stage-left)* Of course, whatever I say.
*(To the* MUSICIAN*)* You can begin now.
   *(The* MUSICIAN *begins playing;* MOMMY *and* DADDY
   *exit; the* MUSICIAN, *all the while playing, nods to the*
   YOUNG MAN*)*


YOUNG MAN
*(With the same endearing smile)* Hi!
   *(After a moment,* MOMMY *and* DADDY *re-enter,
   carrying* GRANDMA. *She is borne in by their hands
   under her armpits; she is quite rigid; her legs are drawn
   up; her feet do not touch the ground; the expression on
   her ancient face is that of puzzlement and fear)*

DADDY
Where do we put her?


MOMMY
*(The same little laugh)* Wherever I say, of course. Let me see
. . . well . . . all right, over there . . . in the sandbox.
*(Pause)* Well, what are you waiting for, Daddy? . . . The
sandbox!
> *(Together they carry* GRANDMA *over to the sandbox
> and more or less dump her in)*


GRANDMA
*(Righting herself to a sitting position; her voice a cross between
a baby's laugh and cry)* Ahhhhhh! Graaaaa!


DADDY *(Dusting himself)*
What do we do now?


MOMMY
*(To the* MUSICIAN*)* You can stop now.
> *(The* MUSICIAN *stops)*
*(Back to* DADDY*)* What do you mean, what do we do now?
We go over there and sit down, of course. *(To the* YOUNG
MAN*)* Hello there.


YOUNG MAN
*(Again smiling)* Hi!
> *(*MOMMY *and* DADDY *move to the chairs, stage-right,
> and sit down. A pause)*


GRANDMA
*(Same as before)* Ahhhhhh! Ah-haaaaaa! Graaaaaa!


DADDY
Do you think . . . do you think she's . . . comfortable?

MOMMY *(Impatiently)*
How would I know?

DADDY
*(Pause)* What do we do now?

MOMMY
*(As if remembering)* We . . . wait. We . . . sit here . . . and
we wait . . . that's what we do.

DADDY
*(After a pause)* Shall we talk to each other?

MOMMY
*(With that little laugh; picking something off her dress)* Well,
*you* can talk, if you want to . . . if you can think of anything
to *say* . . . if you can think of anything *new*.

DADDY *(Thinks)*
No . . . I suppose not.

MOMMY
*(With a triumphant laugh)* Of course not!

GRANDMA
*(Banging the toy shovel against the pail)* Haaaaaa! Ah-
haaaaaa!

MOMMY
*(Out over the audience)* Be quiet, Grandma . . . just be quiet,
and wait.
          (GRANDMA *throws a shovelful of sand at* MOMMY)

MOMMY

*(Still out over the audience)* She's throwing sand at me! You stop that, Grandma; you stop throwing sand at Mommy! *(To* DADDY) She's throwing sand at me.

(DADDY *looks around at* GRANDMA, *who screams at him)*

GRANDMA

GRAAAAA!

MOMMY

Don't look at her. Just . . . sit here . . . be very still . . . and wait. *(To the* MUSICIAN) You . . . uh . . . you go ahead and do whatever it is you do.

*(The* MUSICIAN *plays)*

(MOMMY *and* DADDY *are fixed, staring out beyond the audience.* GRANDMA *looks at them, looks at the* MUSICIAN, *looks at the sandbox, throws down the shovel)*

GRANDMA

Ah-haaaaaa! Graaaaaa! *(Looks for reaction; gets none. Now . . . directly to the audience)* Honestly! What a way to treat an old woman! Drag her out of the house . . . stick her in a car . . . bring her out here from the city . . . dump her in a pile of sand . . . and leave her here to set. I'm eighty-six years old! I was married when I was seventeen. To a farmer. He died when I was thirty. *(To the* MUSICIAN) Will you stop that, please?

*(The* MUSICIAN *stops playing)*

I'm a feeble old woman . . . how do you expect anybody to hear me over that peep! peep! peep! *(To herself)* There's no respect around here. *(To the* YOUNG MAN) There's no respect around here!

YOUNG MAN

*(Same smile)* Hi!


GRANDMA

*(After a pause, a mild double-take, continues, to the audience)*
My husband died when I was thirty *(indicates* MOMMY*),* and I
had to raise that big cow over there all by my lonesome. You
can imagine what *that* was like. Lordy! *(To the* YOUNG MAN*)*
Where'd they get *you?*


YOUNG MAN

Oh . . . I've been around for a while.


GRANDMA

I'll bet you have! Heh, heh, heh. Will you look at you!


YOUNG MAN

*(Flexing his muscles)* Isn't that something? *(Continues his
calisthenics)*


GRANDMA

Boy, oh boy; I'll say. Pretty good.


YOUNG MAN *(Sweetly)*

I'll say.


GRANDMA

Where ya from?


YOUNG MAN

Southern California.

GRANDMA *(Nodding)*
Figgers, figgers. What's your name, honey?


YOUNG MAN
I don't know. . . .


GRANDMA
*(To the audience)* Bright, too!


YOUNG MAN
I mean . . . I mean, they haven't given me one yet . . . the studio . . .


GRANDMA
*(Giving him the once-over)* You don't say . . . you don't say. Well . . . uh, I've got to talk some more . . . don't you go 'way.


YOUNG MAN
Oh, no.


GRANDMA
*(Turning her attention back to the audience)* Fine; fine. *(Then, once more, back to the* YOUNG MAN*)* You're . . . you're an actor, hunh?


YOUNG MAN *(Beaming)*
Yes. I am.


GRANDMA
*(To the audience again; shrugs)* I'm smart that way. *Anyhow,* I had to raise . . . *that* over there all by my lonesome; and

what's next to her there . . . that's what she married. Rich? I tell you . . . money, money, money. They took me off the *farm* . . . which was real decent of them . . . and they moved me into the big town house with *them* . . . fixed a nice place for me under the stove . . . gave me an army blanket . . . and my own dish . . . my very own dish! So, what have I got to complain about? Nothing, of course. I'm not complaining. *(She looks up at the sky, shouts to someone off stage)* Shouldn't it be getting dark now, dear?
> *(The lights dim; night comes on. The* MUSICIAN *begins to play; it becomes deepest night. There are spots on all the players, including the* YOUNG MAN, *who is, of course, continuing his calisthenics)*

DADDY *(Stirring)*

It's nighttime.

MOMMY

Shhhh. Be still . . . wait.

DADDY *(Whining)*

It's so hot.

MOMMY

Shhhhhh. Be still . . . wait.

GRANDMA

*(To herself)* That's better. Night. *(To the* MUSICIAN*)* Honey, do you play all through this part?
> *(The* MUSICIAN *nods)*

Well, keep it nice and soft; that's a good boy.
> *(The* MUSICIAN *nods again; plays softly)*

That's nice.
> *(There is an off-stage rumble)*

DADDY *(Starting)*

What was that?


MOMMY

*(Beginning to weep)* It was nothing.


DADDY

It was . . . it was . . . thunder . . . or a wave breaking . . . or
something.


MOMMY

*(Whispering, through her tears)* It was an off-stage rumble . . .
and you know what *that* means. . . .


DADDY

I forget. . . .


MOMMY

*(Barely able to talk)* It means the time has come for poor
Grandma . . . and I can't bear it!


DADDY *(Vacantly)*

I . . . I suppose you've got to be brave.


GRANDMA *(Mocking)*

That's right, kid; be brave. You'll bear up; you'll get over it.
            *(Another off-stage rumble . . . louder)*


MOMMY

Ohhhhhhhhhh . . . poor Grandma . . . poor Grandma. . . .


GRANDMA *(To* MOMMY*)*

I'm fine! I'm all right! It hasn't happened yet!

*(A violent off-stage rumble. All the lights go out, save the spot on the* YOUNG MAN; *the* MUSICIAN *stops playing)*

MOMMY

Ohhhhhhhhhh. . . . Ohhhhhhhhhh. . . .

*(Silence)*

GRANDMA

Don't put the lights up yet . . . I'm not ready; I'm not quite ready. *(Silence)* All right, dear . . . I'm about done.
*(The lights come up again, to brightest day; the* MUSICIAN *begins to play.* GRANDMA *is discovered, still in the sandbox, lying on her side, propped up on an elbow, half covered, busily shoveling sand over herself)*

GRANDMA *(Muttering)*

I don't know how I'm supposed to do anything with this goddam toy shovel. . . .

DADDY

Mommy! It's daylight!

MOMMY *(Brightly)*

So it is! Well! Our long night is over. We must put away our tears, take off our mourning . . . and face the future. It's our duty.

GRANDMA

*(Still shoveling; mimicking)* . . . take off our mourning . . . face the future. . . . Lordy!

(MOMMY *and* DADDY *rise, stretch.* MOMMY *waves to the* YOUNG MAN)

YOUNG MAN

*(With that smile)* Hi!
(GRANDMA *plays dead.* (!) MOMMY *and* DADDY *go over to look at her; she is a little more than half buried in the sand; the toy shovel is in her hands, which are crossed on her breast)*

MOMMY

*(Before the sandbox; shaking her head)* Lovely! It's . . . it's hard to be sad . . . she looks . . . so happy. *(With pride and conviction)* It pays to do things well. *(To the* MUSICIAN*)* All right, you can stop now, if you want to. I mean, stay around for a swim, or something; it's all right with us. *(She sighs heavily)* Well, Daddy . . . off we go.

DADDY

Brave Mommy!

MOMMY

Brave Daddy!
*(They exit, stage-left)*

GRANDMA

*(After they leave; lying quite still)* It pays to do things well. . . . Boy, oh boy! *(She tries to sit up)* . . . well, kids . . . *(but she finds she can't)* . . . I . . . I can't get up. I . . . I can't move. . . .
*(The* YOUNG MAN *stops his calisthenics, nods to the* MUSICIAN, *walks over to* GRANDMA, *kneels down by the sandbox)*

GRANDMA

I . . . can't move. . . .

YOUNG MAN

Shhhhh . . . be very still. . . .

GRANDMA

I . . . I can't move. . . .

YOUNG MAN

Uh . . . ma'am; I . . . I have a line here.

GRANDMA

Oh, I'm sorry, sweetie; you go right ahead.

YOUNG MAN

I am . . . uh . . .

GRANDMA

Take your time, dear.

YOUNG MAN

*(Prepares; delivers the line like a real amateur)* I am the Angel
of Death. I am . . . uh . . . I am come for you.

GRANDMA

What . . . wha . . . *(Then, with resignation)* . . . ohhhh . . .
ohhhh, I see.
              *(The* YOUNG MAN *bends over, kisses* GRANDMA *gently
              on the forehead)*

GRANDMA
*(Her eyes closed, her hands folded on her breast again,
the shovel between her hands, a sweet smile on her
face)*
Well . . . that was very nice, dear. . . .

YOUNG MAN
*(Still kneeling)* Shhhhhh . . . be still. . . .

GRANDMA
What I meant was . . . you did that very well, dear. . . .

YOUNG MAN *(Blushing)*
. . . oh . . .

GRANDMA
No; I mean it. You've got that . . . you've got a quality.

YOUNG MAN
*(With his endearing smile)* Oh . . . thank you; thank you very
much . . . ma'am.

GRANDMA
*(Slowly; softly—as the* YOUNG MAN *puts his hands on top of*
GRANDMA'S*)* You're . . . you're welcome . . . dear.
*(Tableau. The* MUSICIAN *continues to play as the
curtain slowly comes down)*

# CURTAIN

# *The American Dream*

A PLAY IN ONE SCENE (1959–1960)

For David Diamond

FIRST PERFORMANCE
January 24, 1961, New York City.

York Playhouse.

# THE PLAYERS

MOMMY

DADDY

GRANDMA

MRS. BARKER

YOUNG MAN

# THE SCENE

*A living room. Two armchairs, one toward either side of the stage, facing each other diagonally out toward the audience. Against the rear wall, a sofa. A door, leading out from the apartment, in the rear wall, far stage-right. An archway, leading to other rooms, in the side wall, stage-left.*

At *the beginning,* MOMMY *and* DADDY *are seated in the armchairs,* DADDY *in the armchair stage-left,* MOMMY *in the other.*
    *Curtain up. A silence. Then:*

MOMMY
I don't know what can be keeping them.

DADDY
They're late, naturally.

MOMMY
Of course, they're late; it never fails.

DADDY
That's the way things are today, and there's nothing you can do about it.

MOMMY
You're quite right.

DADDY
When we took this apartment, they were quick enough to have me sign the lease; they were quick enough to take my check for two months' rent in advance . . .

MOMMY
And one month's security . . .

DADDY

. . . and one month's security. They were quick enough to check my references; they were quick enough about all that. But now! But now, try to get the icebox fixed, try to get the doorbell fixed, try to get the leak in the johnny fixed! Just try it . . . they aren't so quick about *that*.

MOMMY

Of course not; it never fails. People think they can get away with anything these days . . . and, of course they can. I went to buy a new hat yesterday.
      (*Pause*)
I said, I went to buy a new hat yesterday.

DADDY

Oh! Yes . . . yes.

MOMMY

Pay attention.

DADDY

I *am* paying attention, Mommy.

MOMMY

Well, be sure you do.

DADDY

Oh, I am.

MOMMY

All right, Daddy; now listen.

DADDY

I'm listening, Mommy.

MOMMY
You're sure!


DADDY
Yes . . . yes, I'm sure. I'm all ears.


MOMMY
*(Giggles at the thought; then)*
All right, now. I went to buy a new hat yesterday and I said,
"I'd like a new hat, please." And so, they showed me a few
hats, green ones and blue ones, and I didn't like any of them,
not one bit. What did I say? What did I just say?


DADDY
You didn't like any of them, not one bit.


MOMMY
That's right; you just keep paying attention. And then they
showed me one that I did like. It was a lovely little hat, and I
said, "Oh, this is a lovely little hat; I'll take this hat; oh my, it's
lovely. What color is it?" And they said, "Why, this is beige;
isn't it a lovely little beige hat?" And I said, "Oh, it's just
lovely." And so, I bought it.
*(Stops, looks at* DADDY*)*


DADDY
*(To show he is paying attention)*
And so you bought it.


MOMMY
And so I bought it, and I walked out of the store with the hat
right on my head, and I ran spang into the chairman of our
woman's club, and she said, "Oh, my dear, isn't that a lovely

little hat? Where did you get that lovely little hat? It's the loveliest little hat; I've always wanted a wheat-colored hat *myself.*" And, I said, "Why, no, my dear; this hat is beige; beige." And she laughed and said, "Why no, my dear, that's a wheat-colored hat . . . wheat. I know beige from wheat." And I said, "Well, my dear, I know beige from wheat, too." What did I say? What did I just say?

DADDY
*(Tonelessly)*
Well, my dear, I know beige from wheat, too.

MOMMY
That's right. And she laughed, and she said, "Well, my dear, they certainly put one over on you. That's wheat if I ever saw wheat. But it's lovely, just the same." And then she walked off. She's a dreadful woman, you don't know her; she has dreadful taste, two dreadful children, a dreadful house, and an absolutely adorable husband who sits in a wheel chair all the time. You don't know him. You don't know anybody, do you? She's just a dreadful woman, but she *is* chairman of our woman's club, so naturally I'm terribly fond of her. So, I went right back into the hat shop, and I said, "Look here; what do you mean selling me a hat that you say is beige, when it's wheat all the time . . . wheat! I can tell beige from wheat any day in the week, but not in this artificial light of yours." They have artificial light, Daddy.

DADDY
Have they!

MOMMY
And I said, "The minute I got outside I could tell that it wasn't a beige hat at all; it was a wheat hat." And they said to

me, "How could you tell that when you had the hat on the top of your head?" Well, that made me angry, and so I made a scene right there; I screamed as hard as I could; I took my hat off and I threw it down on the counter, and oh, I made a terrible scene. I said, I made a terrible scene.

DADDY

 *(Snapping to)*
Yes . . . yes . . . good for you!

MOMMY

And I made an absolutely terrible scene; and they became frightened, and they said, "Oh, madam; oh, madam." But I kept right on, and finally they admitted that they might have made a mistake; so they took my hat into the back, and then they came out again with a hat that looked exactly like it. I took one look at it, and I said, "This hat is wheat-colored; wheat." Well, of course, they said, "Oh, no, madam, this hat is beige; you go outside and see." So, I went outside, and lo and behold, it *was* beige. So I bought it.

DADDY

 *(Clearing his throat)*
I would imagine that it was the same hat they tried to sell you before.

MOMMY

 *(With a little laugh)*
Well, of course it was!

DADDY

That's the way things are today; you just can't get satisfaction; you just try.

MOMMY

Well, *I* got satisfaction.


DADDY

That's right, Mommy. You *did* get satisfaction, didn't you?


MOMMY

Why are they so late? I don't know what can be keeping them.


DADDY

I've been trying for two weeks to have the leak in the johnny fixed.


MOMMY

You can't get satisfaction; just try. *I* can get satisfaction, but you can't.


DADDY

I've been trying for two weeks and it isn't so much for my sake; I can always go to the club.


MOMMY

It isn't so much for my sake, either; I can always go shopping.


DADDY

It's really for Grandma's sake.


MOMMY

Of course it's for Grandma's sake. Grandma cries every time she goes to the johnny as it is; but now that it doesn't work it's even worse, it makes Grandma think she's getting feeble-headed.

DADDY
Grandma *is* getting feeble-headed.


MOMMY
Of course Grandma is getting feeble-headed, but not about her johnny-do's.


DADDY
No; that's true. I must have it fixed.


MOMMY
WHY are they so late? I don't know what can be keeping them.


DADDY
When they came here the first time, they were ten minutes early; they were quick enough about it then.
(Enter GRANDMA *from the archway, stage left. She is loaded down with boxes, large and small, neatly wrapped and tied.*)


MOMMY
Why Grandma, look at you! What *is* all that you're carrying?


GRANDMA
They're boxes. What do they look like?


MOMMY
Daddy! Look at Grandma; look at all the boxes she's carrying!


DADDY
My goodness, Grandma; look at all those boxes.

GRANDMA

Where'll I put them?

MOMMY

Heavens! I don't know. Whatever are they for?

GRANDMA

That's nobody's damn business.

MOMMY

Well, in that case, put them down next to Daddy; there.

GRANDMA

(Dumping the boxes down, on and around DADDY'S feet)

I sure wish you'd get the john fixed.

DADDY

Oh, I do wish they'd come and fix it. We hear you . . . for hours . . . whimpering away. . . .

MOMMY

Daddy! What a terrible thing to say to Grandma!

GRANDMA

Yeah. For shame, talking to me that way.

DADDY

I'm sorry, Grandma.

MOMMY

Daddy's sorry, Grandma.

GRANDMA

Well, all right. In that case I'll go get the rest of the boxes. I suppose I deserve being talked to that way. I've gotten so old. Most people think that when you get so old, you either freeze to death, or you burn up. But you don't. When you get so old, all that happens is that people talk to you that way.

DADDY
*(Contrite)*
I said I'm sorry, Grandma.

MOMMY
Daddy said he was sorry.

GRANDMA

Well, that's all that counts. People being sorry. Makes you feel better; gives you a sense of dignity, and that's all that's important . . . a sense of dignity. And it doesn't matter if you don't care, or not, either. You got to have a sense of dignity, even if you don't care, 'cause, if you don't have that, civilization's doomed.

MOMMY
You've been reading my book club selections again!

DADDY
How dare you read Mommy's book club selections, Grandma!

GRANDMA

Because I'm old! When you're old you gotta do something. When you get old, you can't talk to people because people snap at you. When you get so old, people talk to you that way. That's why you become deaf, so you won't be able to hear

people talking to you that way. And that's why you go and
hide under the covers in the big soft bed, so you won't feel the
house shaking from people talking to you that way. That's
why old people die, eventually. People talk to them that way.
I've got to go and get the rest of the boxes.
    (GRANDMA *exits*)


                        DADDY
Poor Grandma, I didn't mean to hurt her.


                        MOMMY
Don't you worry about it; Grandma doesn't know what she
means.


                        DADDY
She knows what she says, though.


                        MOMMY
Don't you worry about it; she won't know that soon. I love
Grandma.


                        DADDY
I love her, too. Look how nicely she wrapped these boxes.


                        MOMMY
Grandma has always wrapped boxes nicely. When I was a
little girl, I was very poor, and Grandma was very poor, too,
because Grandpa was in heaven. And every day, when I went
to school, Grandma used to wrap a box for me, and I used to
take it with me to school; and when it was lunchtime, all the
little boys and girls used to take out their boxes of lunch, and
they weren't wrapped nicely at all, and they used to open
them and eat their chicken legs and chocolate cakes; and I

used to say, "Oh, look at my lovely lunch box; it's so nicely wrapped it would break my heart to open it." And so, I wouldn't open it.


DADDY

Because it was empty.


MOMMY

Oh no. Grandma always filled it up, because she never ate the dinner she cooked the evening before; she gave me all her food for my lunch box the next day. After school, I'd take the box back to Grandma, and she'd open it and eat the chicken legs and chocolate cake that was inside. Grandma used to say, "I love day-old cake." That's where the expression day-old cake came from. Grandma always ate everything a day late. I used to eat all the other little boys' and girls' food at school, because they thought my lunch box was empty. They thought my lunch box was empty, and that's why I wouldn't open it. They thought I suffered from the sin of pride, and since that made them better than me, they were very generous.


DADDY

You were a very deceitful little girl.


MOMMY

We were very poor! But then I married you, Daddy, and now we're very rich.


DADDY

Grandma isn't rich.


MOMMY

No, but you've been so good to Grandma she feels rich. She doesn't know you'd like to put her in a nursing home.

DADDY

I wouldn't!

MOMMY

Well, heaven knows, *I* would! I can't stand it, watching her do the cooking and the housework, polishing the silver, moving the furniture. . . .

DADDY

She likes to do that. She says it's the least she can do to earn her keep.

MOMMY

Well, she's right. You can't live off people. I can live off you, because I married you. And aren't you lucky all I brought with me was Grandma. A lot of women I know would have brought their whole families to live off you. All I brought was Grandma. Grandma is all the family I have.

DADDY

I feel very fortunate.

MOMMY

You should. I have a right to live off of you because I married you, and because I used to let you get on top of me and bump your uglies; and I have a right to all your money when you die. And when you do, Grandma and I can live by ourselves . . . if she's still here. Unless you have her put away in a nursing home.

DADDY

I have no intention of putting her in a nursing home.

MOMMY

Well, I wish somebody would do something with her!


DADDY

At any rate, you're very well provided for.


MOMMY

You're my sweet Daddy; that's very nice.


DADDY

I love my Mommy.
(*Enter* GRANDMA *again, laden with more boxes*)


GRANDMA
(*Dumping the boxes on and around* DADDY's *feet*)
There; that's the lot of them.


DADDY

They're wrapped so nicely.


GRANDMA
(*To* DADDY)
You won't get on my sweet side that way . . .


MOMMY

Grandma!


GRANDMA

. . . telling me how nicely I wrap boxes. Not after what you
said: how I whimpered for hours. . . .


MOMMY

Grandma!

GRANDMA

(To MOMMY)
Shut up!
(To DADDY)
You don't have any feelings, that's what's wrong with you.
Old people make all sorts of noises, half of them they can't
help. Old people whimper, and cry, and belch, and make
great hollow rumbling sounds at the table; old people wake up
in the middle of the night screaming, and find out they
haven't even been asleep; and when old people *are* asleep,
they try to wake up, and they can't . . . not for the longest
time.

MOMMY

Homilies, homilies!

GRANDMA

And there's more, too.

DADDY

I'm really very sorry, Grandma.

GRANDMA

I know you are, Daddy; it's Mommy over there makes all the
trouble. If you'd listened to me, you wouldn't have married
her in the first place. She was a tramp and a trollop and a trull
to boot, and she's no better now.

MOMMY

Grandma!

GRANDMA

(To MOMMY)
Shut up!

(To DADDY)
When she was no more than eight years old she used to climb
up on my lap and say, in a sickening little voice, "When I
gwo up, I'm going to mahwy a wich old man; I'm going to set
my wittle were end right down in a tub o' butter, that's what
I'm going to do." And I warned you, Daddy; I told you to stay
away from her type. I told you to. I did.

MOMMY
You stop that! You're my mother, not his!

GRANDMA
I am?

DADDY
That's right, Grandma. Mommy's right.

GRANDMA
Well, how would you expect somebody as old as I am to
remember a thing like that? You don't make allowances for
people. I want an allowance. I want an allowance!

DADDY
All right, Grandma; I'll see to it.

MOMMY
Grandma! I'm ashamed of you.

GRANDMA
Humf! It's a fine time to say that. You should have gotten rid
of me a long time ago if that's the way you feel. You should
have had Daddy set me up in business somewhere . . . I
could have gone into the fur business, or I could have been a

singer. But no; not you. You wanted me around so you could
sleep in my room when Daddy got fresh. But now it isn't
important, because Daddy doesn't want to get fresh with you
any more, and I don't blame him. You'd rather sleep with
me, wouldn't you, Daddy?

MOMMY

Daddy doesn't want to sleep with anyone. Daddy's been sick.

DADDY

I've been sick. I don't even want to sleep in the apartment.

MOMMY

You see? I told you.

DADDY

I just want to get everything over with.

MOMMY

That's right. Why are they so late? Why can't they get here on
time?

GRANDMA

(An owl)
Who? Who? . . . Who? Who?

MOMMY

You know, Grandma.

GRANDMA

No, I don't.

MOMMY

Well, it doesn't really matter whether you do or not.

DADDY

Is that true?

MOMMY

Oh, more or less. Look how pretty Grandma wrapped these boxes.

GRANDMA

I didn't really like wrapping them; it hurt my fingers, and it frightened me. But it had to be done.

MOMMY

Why, Grandma?

GRANDMA

None of your damn business.

MOMMY

Go to bed.

GRANDMA

I don't want to go to bed. I just got up. I want to stay here and watch. Besides . . .

MOMMY

Go to bed.

DADDY

Let her stay up, Mommy; it isn't noon yet.

GRANDMA

I want to watch; besides . . .

DADDY

Let her watch, Mommy.

MOMMY

Well all right, you can watch; but don't you dare say a word.

GRANDMA

Old people are very good at listening; old people don't like to talk; old people have colitis and lavender perfume. Now I'm going to be quiet.

DADDY

She never mentioned she wanted to be a singer.

MOMMY

Oh, I forgot to tell you, but it was ages ago.
*(The doorbell rings)*
Oh, goodness! Here they are!

GRANDMA

Who? Who?

MOMMY

Oh, just some people.

GRANDMA

The van people? Is it the van people? Have you finally done it? Have you called the van people to come and take me away?

DADDY

Of course not, Grandma!

GRANDMA

Oh, don't be too sure. She'd have you carted off too, if she thought she could get away with it.

MOMMY

Pay no attention to her, Daddy.
*An aside to* GRANDMA)
My God, you're ungrateful!
*(The doorbell rings again)*

DADDY

*(Wringing his hands)*
Oh dear; oh dear.

MOMMY

*(Still to* GRANDMA)
Just you wait; I'll fix your wagon.
*(Now, to* DADDY)
Well, go let them in, Daddy. What are you waiting for?

DADDY

I think we should talk about it some more. Maybe we've been hasty . . . a little hasty, perhaps.
*(Doorbell rings again)*
I'd like to talk about it some more.

MOMMY

There's no need. You made up your mind; you were firm; you were masculine and decisive.

DADDY

We might consider the pros and the . . .

MOMMY

I won't argue with you; it has to be done; you were right. Open the door.

DADDY

But I'm not sure that . . .

MOMMY

Open the door.

DADDY

Was I firm about it?

MOMMY

Oh, so firm; so firm.

DADDY

And was I decisive?

MOMMY

SO decisive! Oh, I shivered.

DADDY

And masculine? Was I really masculine?

MOMMY

Oh, Daddy, you were so masculine; I shivered and fainted.

GRANDMA
Shivered and fainted, did she? Humf!

MOMMY
You be quiet.

GRANDMA
Old people have a right to talk to themselves; it doesn't hurt
the gums, and it's comforting.
*(Doorbell rings again)*

DADDY
*(Backing off from the door)*
Maybe we can send them away.

MOMMY
Oh, look at you! You're turning into jelly; you're indecisive;
you're a woman.

DADDY
All right. Watch me now; I'm going to open the door. Watch.
Watch!

MOMMY
We're watching; we're watching.

GRANDMA
*I'm* not.

DADDY
Watch now; it's opening.
*(He opens the door)*
It's open!

(MRS. BARKER *steps into the room*)
Here they are!

MOMMY

Here they are!

GRANDMA

Where?

DADDY

Come in. You're late. But, of course, we expected you to be
late; we were saying that we expected you to be late.

MOMMY

Daddy, don't be rude! We were saying that you just can't get
satisfaction these days, and we were talking about you, of
course. Won't you come in?

MRS. BARKER

Thank you. I don't mind if I do.

MOMMY

We're very glad that you're here, late as you are. You do
remember us, don't you? You were here once before. I'm
Mommy, and this is Daddy, and that's Grandma, doddering
there in the corner.

MRS. BARKER

Hello, Mommy; hello, Daddy; and hello there, Grandma.

DADDY

Now that you're here, I don't suppose you could go away and
maybe come back some other time.

MRS. BARKER

Oh no; we're much too efficient for that. I said, hello there, Grandma.

MOMMY

Speak to them, Grandma.

GRANDMA

I don't see them.

DADDY

For shame, Grandma; they're here.

MRS. BARKER

Yes, we're here, Grandma. I'm Mrs. Barker. I remember you; don't you remember me?

GRANDMA

I don't recall. Maybe you were younger, or something.

MOMMY

Grandma! What a terrible thing to say!

MRS. BARKER

Oh now, don't scold her, Mommy; for all she knows she may be right.

DADDY

Uh . . . Mrs. Barker, is it? Won't you sit down?

MRS. BARKER

I don't mind if I do.

MOMMY
Would you like a cigarette, and a drink, and would you like to
cross your legs?

MRS. BARKER
You forget yourself, Mommy; I'm a professional woman. But
I will cross my legs.

DADDY
Yes, make yourself comfortable.

MRS. BARKER
I don't mind if I do.

GRANDMA
Are they still here?

MOMMY
Be quiet, Grandma.

MRS. BARKER
Oh, we're still here. My, what an unattractive apartment you
have!

MOMMY
Yes, but you don't know what a trouble it is. Let me tell
you . . .

DADDY
I was saying to Mommy . . .

MRS. BARKER
Yes, I know. I was listening outside.

DADDY

About the icebox, and . . . the doorbell . . . and the . . .


MRS. BARKER

. . . and the johnny. Yes, we're very efficient; we have to
know everything in our work.


DADDY

Exactly what do you do?


MOMMY

Yes, what is your work?


MRS. BARKER

Well, my dear, for one thing, I'm chairman of your woman's
club.


MOMMY

Don't be ridiculous. I was talking to the chairman of my
woman's club just yester— Why, so you are. You remember,
Daddy, the lady I was telling you about? The lady with the
husband who sits in the *swing?* Don't you remember?


DADDY

No . . . no. . . .


MOMMY

Of course you do. I'm so sorry, Mrs. Barker. I would have
known you anywhere, except in this artificial light. And look!
You have a hat just like the one I bought yesterday.


MRS. BARKER
*(With a little laugh)*
No, not really; this hat is cream.

MOMMY

Well, my dear, that may look like a cream hat to you, but I can . . .


MRS. BARKER

Now, now; you seem to forget who I am.


MOMMY

Yes, I do, don't I? Are you sure you're comfortable? Won't you take off your dress?


MRS. BARKER

I don't mind if I do.
*(She removes her dress)*


MOMMY

There. You must feel a great deal more comfortable.


MRS. BARKER

Well, I certainly *look* a great deal more comfortable.


DADDY

I'm going to blush and giggle.


MOMMY

Daddy's going to blush and giggle.


MRS. BARKER

*(Pulling the hem of her slip above her knees)*
You're lucky to have such a man for a husband.


MOMMY

Oh, don't I know it!

DADDY

I just blushed and giggled and went sticky wet.

MOMMY

Isn't Daddy a caution, Mrs. Barker?

MRS. BARKER

Maybe if I smoked . . . ?

MOMMY

Oh, that isn't necessary.

MRS. BARKER

I don't mind if I do.

MOMMY

No; no, don't. Really.

MRS. BARKER

I don't mind . . .

MOMMY

I won't have you smoking in my house, and that's that! You're a professional woman.

DADDY

Grandma drinks AND smokes; don't you, Grandma?

GRANDMA

No.

MOMMY

Well, now, Mrs. Barker; suppose you tell us why you're here.

GRANDMA
*(As* MOMMY *walks through the boxes)*
The boxes . . . the boxes . . .


MOMMY
Be quiet, Grandma.


DADDY
What did you say, Grandma!


GRANDMA
*(As* MOMMY *steps on several of the boxes)*
The boxes, damn it!


MRS. BARKER
Boxes; she said boxes. She mentioned the boxes.


DADDY
What about the boxes, Grandma? Maybe Mrs. Barker is here
because of the boxes. Is that what you meant, Grandma?


GRANDMA
I don't know if that's what I meant or not. It's certainly not
what I *thought* I meant.


DADDY
Grandma is of the opinion that . . .


MRS. BARKER
Can we assume that the boxes are for us? I mean, can we
assume that you had us come here for the boxes?

MOMMY
Are you in the habit of receiving boxes?

DADDY
A very good question.

MRS. BARKER
Well, that would depend on the reason we're here. I've got my fingers in so many little pies, you know. Now, I can think of one of my little activities in which we are in the habit of receiving *baskets*; but more in a literary sense than really. We *might* receive boxes, though, under very special circumstances. I'm afraid that's the best answer I can give you.

DADDY
It's a very interesting answer.

MRS. BARKER
*I* thought so. But, does it help?

MOMMY
No; I'm afraid not.

DADDY
I wonder if it might help us any if I said I feel misgivings, that I have definite qualms.

MOMMY
Where, Daddy?

DADDY
Well, mostly right here, right around where the stitches were.

MOMMY
Daddy had an operation, you know.

MRS. BARKER
Oh, you poor Daddy! I didn't know; but then, how could I?

GRANDMA
You might have asked; it wouldn't have hurt you.

MOMMY
Dry up, Grandma.

GRANDMA
There you go. Letting your true feelings come out. Old people aren't dry enough, I suppose. My sacks are empty, the fluid in my eyeballs is all caked on the inside edges, my spine is made of sugar candy, I breathe ice; but you don't hear me complain. Nobody hears old people complain because people think that's all old people do. And *that's* because old people are gnarled and sagged and twisted into the shape of a complaint.
        (*Signs off*)
That's all.

MRS. BARKER
What was wrong, Daddy?

DADDY
Well, you know how it is: the doctors took out something that was there and put in something that wasn't there. An operation.

MRS. BARKER
You're very fortunate, I should say.


MOMMY
Oh, he is; he is. All his life, Daddy has wanted to be a United
States Senator; but now . . . why now he's changed his mind,
and for the rest of his life he's going to want to be Governor
. . . it would be nearer the apartment, you know.


MRS. BARKER
You *are* fortunate, Daddy.


DADDY
Yes, indeed; except that I get these qualms now and then,
definite ones.


MRS. BARKER
Well, it's just a matter of things settling; you're like an old
house.


MOMMY
Why Daddy, thank Mrs. Barker.


DADDY
Thank you.


MRS. BARKER
Ambition! That's the ticket. I have a brother who's very much
like you, Daddy . . . ambitious. Of course, he's a great deal
younger than you; he's even younger than I am . . . if such a
thing is possible. He runs a little newspaper. Just a little
newspaper . . . but he runs it. He's chief cook and bottle

washer of that little newspaper, which he calls *The Village Idiot*. He has such a sense of humor; he's so self-deprecating, so modest. And he'd never admit it himself, but he *is* the Village Idiot.

MOMMY

Oh, I think that's just grand. Don't you think so, Daddy?

DADDY

Yes, just grand.

MRS. BARKER

My brother's a dear man, and he has a dear little wife, whom he loves, dearly. He loves her so much he just can't get a sentence out without mentioning her. He wants everybody to know he's married. He's really a stickler on that point; he can't be introduced to anybody and say hello without adding, "Of course, I'm married." As far as I'm concerned, he's the chief exponent of Woman Love in this whole country; he's even been written up in psychiatric journals because of it.

DADDY

Indeed!

MOMMY

Isn't that lovely.

MRS. BARKER

Oh, I think so. There's too much woman hatred in this country, and that's a fact.

GRANDMA

Oh, I don't know.

MOMMY

Oh, I think that's just grand. Don't you think so, Daddy?

DADDY

Yes, just grand.

GRANDMA

In case anybody's interested . . .

MOMMY

Be quiet, Grandma.

GRANDMA

Nuts!

MOMMY

Oh, Mrs. Barker, you *must* forgive Grandma. She's rural.

MRS. BARKER

I don't mind if I do.

DADDY

Maybe Grandma has something to say.

MOMMY

Nonsense. Old people have nothing to say; and if old people
*did* have something to say, nobody would listen to them.
    (To GRANDMA)
You see? I can pull that stuff just as easy as you can.

GRANDMA

Well, you got the rhythm, but you don't really have the
quality. Besides, you're middle-aged.

MOMMY

I'm proud of it!

GRANDMA

Look. I'll show you how it's really done. Middle-aged people think they can do anything, but the truth is that middle-aged people can't do most things as well as they used to. Middle-aged people think they're special because they're like everybody else. We live in the age of deformity. You see? Rhythm *and* content. You'll learn.

DADDY

I do wish I weren't surrounded by women; I'd like some men around here.

MRS. BARKER

You can say that again!

GRANDMA

I don't hardly count as a woman, so can I say my piece?

MOMMY

Go on. Jabber away.

GRANDMA

It's very simple; the fact is, these boxes don't have anything to do with why this good lady is come to call. Now, if you're interested in knowing why these boxes *are* here . . .

MOMMY

Well, nobody *is* interested!

GRANDMA

You can be as snippety as you like for all the good it'll do you.

DADDY

You two will have to stop arguing.

MOMMY

I don't argue with her.

DADDY

It will just have to stop.

MOMMY

Well, why don't you call a van and have her taken away?

GRANDMA

Don't bother; there's no need.

DADDY

No, now, perhaps I can go away myself. . . .

MOMMY

Well, one or the other; the way things are now it's impossible.
In the first place, it's too crowded in this apartment.
(*To* GRANDMA)
And it's you that takes up all the space, with your enema
bottles, and your Pekinese, and God-only-knows-what-else
. . . and now all these boxes. . . .

GRANDMA

These boxes are . . .

MRS. BARKER

I've never heard of enema *bottles*. . . .

GRANDMA

She means enema bags, but she doesn't know the difference.
Mommy comes from extremely bad stock. And besides, when
Mommy was born . . . well, it was a difficult delivery, and
she had a head shaped like a banana.

MOMMY

You ungrateful—Daddy? Daddy, you see how ungrateful she
is after all these years, after all the things we've done for her?
(*To* GRANDMA)
One of these days you're going away in a van; that's what's
going to happen to you!

GRANDMA

Do tell!

MRS. BARKER

Like a banana?

GRANDMA

Yup, just like a banana.

MRS. BARKER

My word!

MOMMY

You stop listening to her; she'll say anything. Just the other
night she called Daddy a hedgehog.

MRS. BARKER

She didn't!


GRANDMA

That's right, baby; you stick up for me.


MOMMY

I don't know where she gets the words; on the television, maybe.


MRS. BARKER

Did you really call him a hedgehog?


GRANDMA

Oh look; what difference does it make whether I did or not?


DADDY

Grandma's right. Leave Grandma alone.


MOMMY

(To DADDY)
How dare you!


GRANDMA

Oh, leave her alone, Daddy; the kid's all mixed up.


MOMMY

You see? I told you. It's all those television shows. Daddy, you go right into Grandma's room and take her television and shake all the tubes loose.

DADDY

Don't mention tubes to me.

MOMMY

Oh! Mommy forgot!
(To MRS. BARKER)
Daddy has tubes now, where he used to have tracts.

MRS. BARKER

Is that a fact!

GRANDMA

I know why this dear lady is here.

MOMMY

You be still.

MRS. BARKER

Oh, I do wish you'd tell me.

MOMMY

No! No! That wouldn't be fair at all.

DADDY

Besides, she knows why she's here; she's here because we called them.

MRS. BARKER

La! But that still leaves me puzzled. I know I'm here because you called us, but I'm such a busy girl, with this committee and that committee, and the Responsible Citizens Activities I indulge in.

MOMMY

Oh my; busy, busy.


MRS. BARKER

Yes, indeed. So I'm afraid you'll have to give me some help.


MOMMY

Oh, no. No, you must be mistaken. I can't believe we asked you here to give you any help. With the way taxes are these days, and the way you can't get satisfaction in ANYTHING . . . no, I don't believe so.


DADDY

And if you need help . . . why, I should think you'd apply for a Fulbright Scholarship. . . .


MOMMY

And if not that . . . why, then a Guggenheim Fellowship. . . .


GRANDMA

Oh, come on; why not shoot the works and try for the Prix de Rome.
    *(Under her breath to* MOMMY *and* DADDY*)*
Beasts!


MRS. BARKER

Oh, what a jolly family. But let me think. I'm knee-deep in work these days; there's the Ladies' Auxiliary Air Raid Committee, for one thing; how do you feel about air raids?


MOMMY

Oh, I'd say we're hostile.

DADDY

Yes, definitely; we're hostile.

MRS. BARKER

Then, you'll be no help there. There's too much hostility in the world these days as it is; but I'll not badger you! There's a surfeit of badgers as well.

GRANDMA

While we're at it, there's been a run on old people, too. The Department of Agriculture, or maybe it wasn't the Department of Agriculture—anyway, it was some department that's run by a girl—put out figures showing that ninety per cent of the adult population of the country is over eighty years old . . . or eighty per cent is over ninety years old . . .

MOMMY

You're such a liar! You just finished saying that everyone is middle-aged.

GRANDMA

I'm just telling you what the government says . . . that doesn't have anything to do with what . . .

MOMMY

It's that television! Daddy, go break her television.

GRANDMA

You won't find it.

DADDY

(Wearily getting up)

If I must . . . I must.

MOMMY
And don't step on the Pekinese; it's blind.


DADDY
It may be blind, but Daddy isn't.
    *(He exits, through the archway, stage left)*


GRANDMA
You won't find *it*, either.


MOMMY
Oh, I'm so fortunate to have such a husband. Just think: I
could have a husband who was poor, or argumentative, or a
husband who sat in a wheel chair all day . . . OOOOHHHH!
*What* have I said? What *have* I said?


GRANDMA
You said you could have a husband who sat in a wheel . . .


MOMMY
I'm mortified! I could die! I could cut my tongue out!
I could . . .


MRS. BARKER
    *(Forcing a smile)*
Oh, now . . . now . . . don't think about it . . .


MOMMY
I could . . . why, I could . . .


MRS. BARKER
. . . don't think about it . . . really. . . .

MOMMY

You're quite right. I won't think about it, and that way I'll forget that I ever said it, and that way it will be all right.
     *(Pause)*
There . . . I've forgotten. Well, now, now that Daddy is out of the room we can have some girl talk.

MRS. BARKER

I'm not sure that I . . .

MOMMY

You *do* want to have some girl talk, don't you?

MRS. BARKER

I was going to say I'm not sure that I wouldn't care for a glass of water. I feel a little faint.

MOMMY

Grandma, go get Mrs. Barker a glass of water.

GRANDMA

Go get it yourself. I quit.

MOMMY

Grandma loves to do little things around the house; it gives her a false sense of security.

GRANDMA

I quit!-I'm through!

MOMMY

Now, you be a good Grandma, or you know what will happen to you. You'll be taken away in a van.

GRANDMA

You don't frighten me. I'm too old to be frightened. Besides . . .

MOMMY

WELL! I'll tend to you later. I'll hide your teeth . . . I'll . . .

GRANDMA

Everything's hidden.

MRS. BARKER

I *am* going to faint. I *am*.

MOMMY

Good heavens! I'll go myself.
(*As she exits, through the archway, stage-left*)
I'll fix you, Grandma. I'll take care of you later.
(*She exits*)

GRANDMA

Oh, go soak your head.
(*To* MRS. BARKER)
Well, dearie, how do you feel?

MRS. BARKER

A little better, I think. Yes, much better, thank you, Grandma.

GRANDMA

That's good.

MRS. BARKER

But . . . I feel so lost . . . not knowing why I'm here . . . and, on top of it, they say I was here before.

GRANDMA

Well, you were. You weren't *here*, exactly, because we've moved around a lot, from one apartment to another, up and down the social ladder like mice, if you like similes.

MRS. BARKER

I don't . . . particularly.

GRANDMA

Well, then, I'm sorry.

MRS. BARKER

*(Suddenly)*
Grandma, I feel I can trust you.

GRANDMA

Don't be too sure; it's every man for himself around this place. . . .

MRS. BARKER

Oh . . . is it? Nonetheless, I really do feel that I can trust you. *Please* tell me why they called and asked us to come.

GRANDMA

Well, I'll give you a hint. That's the best I can do, because I'm a muddleheaded old woman. Now listen, because it's important. Once upon a time, not too very long ago, but a long enough time ago . . . oh, about twenty years ago . . . there was a man very much like Daddy, and a woman very much like Mommy, who were married to each other, very much like Mommy and Daddy are married to each other; and they lived in an apartment very much like one that's very much like this one, and they lived there with an old woman

who was very much like yours truly, only younger, because it
was some time ago; in fact, they were all somewhat younger.

MRS. BARKER

How fascinating!

GRANDMA

Now, at the same time, there was a dear lady very much like
you, only younger then, who did all sorts of Good
Works. . . . And one of the Good Works this dear lady did
was in something very much like a volunteer capacity for an
organization very much like the Bye-Bye Adoption Service,
which is nearby and which was run by a terribly deaf old lady
very much like the Miss Bye-Bye who runs the Bye-Bye
Adoption Service nearby.

MRS. BARKER

How enthralling!

GRANDMA

Well, be that as it may. Nonetheless, one afternoon this man,
who was very much like Daddy, and this woman who was
very much like Mommy came to see this dear lady who did all
the Good Works, who was very much like you, dear, and they
were very sad and very hopeful, and they cried and smiled and
bit their fingers, and they said all the most intimate things.

MRS. BARKER

How spellbinding! What did they say?

GRANDMA

Well, it was very sweet. The woman, who was very much like
Mommy, said that she and the man who was very much like

Daddy had never been blessed with anything very much like a
bumble of joy.

MRS. BARKER

A what?

GRANDMA

A bumble; a bumble of joy.

MRS. BARKER

Oh, like bundle.

GRANDMA

Well, yes; very much like it. Bundle, bumble; who cares? At
any rate, the woman, who was very much like Mommy, said
that they wanted a bumble of their own, but that the man,
who was very much like Daddy, couldn't have a bumble; and
the man, who was very much like Daddy, said that yes, they
had wanted a bumble of their own, but that the woman, who
was very much like Mommy, couldn't have one, and that
now they wanted to buy something very much like a bumble.

MRS. BARKER

How engrossing!

GRANDMA

Yes. And the dear lady, who was very much like you, said
something that was very much like, "Oh, what a shame; but
take heart . . . I think we have just the bumble *for* you." And,
well, the lady, who was very much like Mommy, and the
man, who was very much like Daddy, cried and smiled and
bit their fingers, and said some more intimate things, which
were totally irrelevant but which were pretty hot stuff, and so
the dear lady, who was very much like you, and who had

something very much like a penchant for pornography, listened with something very much like enthusiasm. "Whee," she said. "Whoooopeeeeee!" But that's beside the point.

MRS. BARKER

I suppose *so*. But how gripping!

GRANDMA

Anyway . . . they *bought* something very much like a bumble, and they took it away with them. But . . . things didn't work out very well.

MRS. BARKER

You mean there was trouble?

GRANDMA

You got it.
      *(With a glance through the archway)*
But, I'm going to have to speed up now because I think I'm leaving soon.

MRS. BARKER

Oh. Are you really?

GRANDMA

Yup.

MRS. BARKER

But old people don't go anywhere; they're either taken places, or put places.

GRANDMA

Well, this old person is different. Anyway . . . things started going badly.

MRS. BARKER

Oh yes. Yes.


GRANDMA

Weeeeellll . . . in the first place, it turned out the bumble didn't look like either one of its parents. That was enough of a blow, but things got worse. One night, it cried its heart out, if you can imagine such a thing.


MRS. BARKER

Cried its heart out! Well!


GRANDMA

But that was only the beginning. Then it turned out it only had eyes for its Daddy.


MRS. BARKER

For its Daddy! Why, any self-respecting woman would have gouged those eyes right out of its head.


GRANDMA

Well, she did. That's exactly what she did. But then, it kept its nose up in the air.


MRS. BARKER

Ufggh! How disgusting!


GRANDMA

That's what they thought. But *then*, it began to develop an interest in its you-know-what.


MRS. BARKER

In its you-know-what! Well! I hope they cut its hands off at the wrists!

GRANDMA

Well, yes, they did that eventually. But first, they cut off its you-know-what.


MRS. BARKER

A much better idea!


GRANDMA

That's what they thought. But after they cut off its you-know-what, it *still* put its hands under the covers, *looking* for its you-know-what. So, finally, they *had* to cut off its hands at the wrists.


MRS. BARKER

Naturally!


GRANDMA

And it was such a resentful bumble. Why, one day it called its Mommy a dirty name.


MRS. BARKER

Well, I hope they cut its tongue out!


GRANDMA

Of course. And then, as it got bigger, they found out all sorts of terrible things about it, like: it didn't have a head on its shoulders, it had no guts, it was spineless, its feet were made of clay . . . just dreadful things.


MRS. BARKER

Dreadful!


GRANDMA

So you can understand how they became discouraged.

MRS. BARKER

I certainly can! And what did they do?

GRANDMA

What did they do? Well, for the last straw, it finally up and
died; and you can imagine how *that* made them feel, their
having paid for it, and all. So, they called up the lady who
sold them the bumble in the first place and told her to come
right over to their apartment. They wanted satisfaction; they
wanted their money back. That's what they wanted.

MRS. BARKER

My, my, my.

GRANDMA

How do you like *them* apples?

MRS. BARKER

My, my, my.

DADDY

*(Off stage)*
Mommy! I can't find Grandma's television, and I can't find
the Pekinese, either.

MOMMY

*(Off stage)*
Isn't that funny! And I can't find the water.

GRANDMA

Heh, heh, heh. I told them everything was hidden.

MRS. BARKER
Did you hide the water, too?


GRANDMA
*(Puzzled)*
No. No, I didn't do *that*.


DADDY
*(Off stage)*
The truth of the matter is, I can't even find Grandma's room.


GRANDMA
Heh, heh, heh.


MRS. BARKER
My! You certainly did hide things, didn't you?


GRANDMA
Sure, kid, sure.


MOMMY
*(Sticking her head in the room)*
Did you ever hear of such a thing, Grandma? Daddy can't
find your television, and he can't find the Pekinese, and the
truth of the matter is he can't even find your room.


GRANDMA
I told you. I hid everything.


MOMMY
Nonsense, Grandma! Just wait until I get my hands on you.
You're a troublemaker . . . that's what you are.

GRANDMA

Well, I'll be out of here pretty soon, baby.

MOMMY

Oh, you don't know how right you are! Daddy's been wanting
to send you away for a long time now, but I've been
restraining him. I'll tell you one thing, though . . . I'm
getting sick and tired of this fighting, and I might just let him
have his way. Then you'll see what'll happen. Away you'll go;
in a van, too. I'll let Daddy call the van man.

GRANDMA

I'm way ahead of you.

MOMMY

How can you be so old and so smug at the same time? You
have no sense of proportion.

GRANDMA

You just answered your own question.

MOMMY

Mrs. Barker, I'd much rather you came into the kitchen for
that glass of water, what with Grandma out here, and all.

MRS. BARKER

I don't see what Grandma has to do with it; and besides, I
don't think you're very polite.

MOMMY

You seem to forget that you're a guest in this house . . .

GRANDMA

Apartment!


MOMMY

Apartment! And that you're a professional woman. So, if you'll be so good as to come into the kitchen, I'll be more than happy to show you where the water is, and where the glass is, and then you can put two and two together, if you're clever enough.
*(She vanishes)*


MRS. BARKER

*(After a moment's consideration)*
I suppose she's right.


GRANDMA

Well, that's how it is when people call you up and ask you over to do something for them.


MRS. BARKER

I suppose you're right, too. Well, Grandma, it's been very nice talking to you.


GRANDMA

And I've enjoyed listening. Say, don't tell Mommy or Daddy that I gave you that hint, will you?


MRS. BARKER

Oh, dear me, the hint! I'd forgotten about it, if you can imagine such a thing. No, I won't breathe a word of it to them.

GRANDMA

I don't know if it helped you any . . .

MRS. BARKER

I can't tell, yet. I'll have to . . . what *is* the word I want? . . .
I'll have to relate it . . . that's it . . . I'll have to relate it to
certain things that I *know*, and . . . draw . . . con-
clusions. . . . What I'll really have to do is to see if it applies
to anything. I mean, after all, I *do* do volunteer work for an
adoption service, but it isn't very much *like* the Bye-Bye
Adoption Service . . . it *is* the Bye-Bye Adoption Service . . .
and while I can remember Mommy and Daddy coming to see
me, oh about twenty years ago, about buying a bumble, I
can't quite remember anyone very much *like* Mommy and
Daddy coming to see me about buying a bumble. Don't you
see? It really presents quite a problem. . . . I'll have to think
about it . . . mull it . . . but at any rate, it was truly first-class
of you to try to help me. Oh, will you still be here after I've
had my drink of water?

GRANDMA

Probably . . . I'm not as spry as I used to be.

MRS. BARKER

Oh. Well, I won't say good-by then.

GRANDMA

No. Don't.
(MRS. BARKER *exits through the archway*)
People don't say good-by to old people because they think
they'll frighten them. Lordy! If they only knew how awful
"hello" and "my, you're looking chipper" sounded, they
wouldn't say those things either. The truth is, there isn't

much you *can* say to old people that doesn't sound just terrible.
>    *(The doorbell rings)*
Come on in!
>    *(The* YOUNG MAN *enters.* GRANDMA *looks him over)*
Well, now, aren't you a breath of fresh air!

YOUNG MAN

Hello there.

GRANDMA

My, my, my. Are you the van man?

YOUNG MAN

The what?

GRANDMA

The van man. The van man. Are you come to take me away?

YOUNG MAN

I don't know what you're talking about.

GRANDMA

Oh.
>    *(Pause)*
Well.
>    *(Pause)*
My, my, aren't you something!

YOUNG MAN

Hm?

GRANDMA

I said, my, my, aren't you something.

YOUNG MAN

Oh. Thank you.

GRANDMA

You don't sound very enthusiastic.

YOUNG MAN

Oh, I'm . . . I'm used to it.

GRANDMA

Yup . . . yup. You know, if I were about a hundred and fifty
years younger I could go for you.

YOUNG MAN

Yes, I imagine so.

GRANDMA

Unh-hunh . . . will you look at those muscles!

YOUNG MAN
*(Flexing his muscles)*
Yes, they're quite good, aren't they?

GRANDMA

Boy, they sure are. They natural?

YOUNG MAN

Well the basic structure was there, but I've done some work,
too . . . you know, in a gym.

GRANDMA

I'll bet you have. You ought to be in the movies, boy.


YOUNG MAN

I know.


GRANDMA

Yup! Right up there on the old silver screen. But I suppose you've heard that before.


YOUNG MAN

Yes, I have.


GRANDMA

You ought to try out for them . . . the movies.


YOUNG MAN

Well, actually, I may have a career there yet. I've lived out on the West Coast almost all my life . . . and I've met a few people who . . . might be able to help me. I'm not in too much of a hurry, though. I'm almost as young as I look.


GRANDMA

Oh, that's nice. And will you look at that face!


YOUNG MAN

Yes, it's quite good, isn't it? Clean-cut, midwest farm boy type, almost insultingly good-looking in a typically American way. Good profile, straight nose, honest eyes, wonderful smile . . .

GRANDMA

Yup. Boy, you know what you are, don't you? You're the
American Dream, that's what you are. All those other people,
they don't know what they're talking about. You . . . *you* are
the American Dream.

YOUNG MAN

Thanks.

MOMMY

*(Off stage)*
Who rang the doorbell?

GRANDMA

*(Shouting off-stage)*
The American Dream!

MOMMY

*(Off stage)*
What? What was that, Grandma?

GRANDMA

*(Shouting)*
The American Dream! The American Dream! Damn it!

DADDY

*(Off stage)*
How's that, Mommy?

MOMMY

*(Off stage)*
Oh, some gibberish; pay no attention. Did you find
Grandma's room?

DADDY
*(Off stage)*
No. I can't even find Mrs. Barker.

YOUNG MAN
What was all that?

GRANDMA
Oh, that was just the folks, but let's not talk about them, honey; let's talk about you.

YOUNG MAN
All right.

GRANDMA
Well, let's see. If you're not the van man, what are you doing here?

YOUNG MAN
I'm looking for work.

GRANDMA
Are you! Well, what kind of work?

YOUNG MAN
Oh, almost anything . . . almost anything that pays. I'll do almost anything for money.

GRANDMA
Will you . . . will you? Hmmmm. I wonder if there's anything you could do around here?

YOUNG MAN

There might be. It looked to be a likely building.

GRANDMA

It's always looked to be a rather unlikely building to me, but I suppose you'd know better than I.

YOUNG MAN

I can sense these things.

GRANDMA

There *might* be something you could do around here. Stay there! Don't come any closer.

YOUNG MAN

Sorry.

GRANDMA

I don't mean I'd *mind*. I don't know whether I'd mind, or not. . . . But it wouldn't look well; it would look just *awful*.

YOUNG MAN

Yes; I suppose so.

GRANDMA

Now, stay there, let me concentrate. What could you do? The folks have been in something of a quandary around here today, sort of a dilemma, and I wonder if you mightn't be some help.

YOUNG MAN

I hope so . . . if there's money in it. Do you have any money?

GRANDMA

Money! Oh, there's more money around here than you'd know what to do with.

YOUNG MAN

I'm not so sure.

GRANDMA

Well, maybe not. Besides, I've got money of my own.

YOUNG MAN

You have?

GRANDMA

Sure. Old people quite often have lots of money; more often than most people expect. Come here, so I can whisper to you . . . not too close. I might faint.

YOUNG MAN

Oh, I'm sorry.

GRANDMA

It's all right, dear. Anyway . . . have you ever heard of that big baking contest they run? The one where all the ladies get together in a big barn and bake away?

YOUNG MAN

I'm . . . not . . . sure. . . .

GRANDMA

Not so close. Well, it doesn't matter whether you've heard of it or not. The important thing is—and I don't want anybody to hear this . . . the folks think I haven't been out of the house in eight years—the important thing is that I won first prize in that baking contest this year. Oh, it was in all the papers; not under my own name, though. I used a *nom de boulangère*; I called myself Uncle Henry.

YOUNG MAN

Did you?

GRANDMA

Why not? I didn't see any reason not to. I look just as much like an old man as I do like an old woman. And you know what I called it . . . what I won for?

YOUNG MAN

No. What did you call it?

GRANDMA

I called it Uncle Henry's Day-Old Cake.

YOUNG MAN

That's a very nice name.

GRANDMA

And it wasn't any trouble, either. All I did was go out and get a store-bought cake, and keep it around for a while, and then slip it in, unbeknownst to anybody. Simple.

YOUNG MAN

You're a very resourceful person.

GRANDMA

Pioneer stock.

YOUNG MAN
Is all this true? Do you want me to believe all this?


GRANDMA
Well, you can believe it or not . . . it doesn't make any difference to me. All *I* know is, Uncle Henry's Day-Old Cake won me twenty-five thousand smackerolas.


YOUNG MAN
Twenty-five thou—


GRANDMA
Right on the old loggerhead. Now . . . how do you like them apples?


YOUNG MAN
Love 'em.


GRANDMA
I thought you'd be impressed.


YOUNG MAN
Money talks.


GRANDMA
Hey! You look familiar.


YOUNG MAN
Hm? Pardon?


GRANDMA
I said, you look familiar.

YOUNG MAN
Well, I've done some modeling.


GRANDMA
No . . . no. I don't mean that. You look familiar.


YOUNG MAN
Well, I'm a type.


GRANDMA
Yup; you sure are. Why do you say you'd do almost anything
for money . . . if you don't mind my being nosy?


YOUNG MAN
No, no. It's part of the interview. I'll be happy to tell you. It's
that I have no talents at all, except what you see . . . my
person; my body, my face. In every other way I am
incomplete, and I must therefore . . . compensate.


GRANDMA
What do you mean, incomplete? You look pretty complete to
me.


YOUNG MAN
I think I can explain it to you, partially because you're very
old, and very old people have perceptions they keep to
themselves, because if they expose them to other people . . .
well, you know what ridicule and neglect are.


GRANDMA
I do, child, I do.


YOUNG MAN
Then listen. My mother died the night that I was born, and I

never knew my father; I doubt my mother did. But, I wasn't alone, because lying with me . . . in the placenta . . . there was someone else . . . my brother . . . my twin.

GRANDMA

Oh, my child.

YOUNG MAN

We were identical twins . . . he and I . . . not fraternal . . . identical; we were derived from the same ovum; and in *this,* in that we were twins not from separate ova but from the same one, we had a kinship such as you cannot imagine. We . . . we felt each other breathe . . . his heartbeats thundered in my temples . . . mine in his . . . our stomachs ached and we cried for feeding at the same time . . . are you old enough to understand?

GRANDMA

I think so, child; I think I'm nearly old enough.

YOUNG MAN

I hope so. But we were separated when we were still very young, my brother, my twin and I . . . inasmuch as you can separate one being. We were torn apart . . . thrown to opposite ends of the continent. I don't know what became of my brother . . . to the rest of myself . . . except that, from time to time, in the years that have passed, I have suffered losses . . . that I can't explain. A fall from grace . . . a departure of innocence . . . loss . . . loss. How can I put it to you? All right; like this: Once . . . it was as if all at once my heart . . . became numb . . . almost as though I . . . almost as though . . . just like that . . . it had been wrenched from my body . . . and from that time I have been unable to love. Once . . . I was asleep at the time . . . I awoke, and my eyes

were burning. And since that time I have been unable to see
anything, *anything*, with pity, with affection . . . with
anything but . . . cool disinterest. And my groin . . . even
there . . . since one time . . . one specific agony . . . since
then I have not been able to *love* anyone with my body. And
even my hands . . . I cannot touch another person and feel
love. And there is more . . . there are more losses, but it all
comes down to this: I no longer have the capacity to feel
anything. I have no emotions. I have been drained, torn
asunder . . . disemboweled. I have, now, only my person
. . . my body, my face. I use what I have . . . I let people love
me . . . I accept the syntax around me, for while I know I
cannot relate . . . I know I must be related *to*. I let people
love me . . . I let people touch me . . . I let them draw
pleasure from my groin . . . from my presence . . . from the
fact of me . . . but, that is all it comes to. As I told you, I am
incomplete . . . I can feel nothing. I can feel nothing. And so
. . . here I am . . . as you see me. I am . . . but this . . .
what you see. And it will always be thus.


GRANDMA

Oh, my child; my child.
        (*Long pause; then*)
I was mistaken . . . before. I don't know you from somewhere, but I knew . . . once . . . someone very much like
you . . . or, very much as perhaps you were.


YOUNG MAN

Be careful; be very careful. What I have told you may not be
true. In my profession . . .


GRANDMA

Shhhhhh.
        (*The* YOUNG MAN *bows his head, in acquiescence*)
Someone . . . to be more precise . . . who might have turned

out to be very much like you might have turned out to be. And . . . unless I'm terribly mistaken . . . you've found yourself a job.

YOUNG MAN

What are my duties?

MRS. BARKER
*(Off stage)*
Yoo-hoo! Yoo-hoo!

GRANDMA

Oh-oh. You'll . . . you'll have to play it by ear, my dear . . . unless I get a chance to talk to you again. I've got to go into my act, now.

YOUNG MAN

But, I . . .

GRANDMA

Yoo-hoo!

MRS. BARKER
*(Coming through archway)*
Yoo-hoo . . . oh, there you are, Grandma. I'm glad to see somebody. I can't find Mommy or Daddy.
*(Double takes)*
Well . . . who's this?

GRANDMA

This? Well . . . uh . . . oh, this is the . . . uh . . . the van man. That's who it is . . . the van man.

MRS. BARKER

So! It's true! They *did* call the van man. They *are* having you
carted away.

GRANDMA

*(Shrugging)*
Well, you know. It figures.

MRS. BARKER

*(To YOUNG MAN)*
How dare you cart this poor old woman away!

YOUNG MAN

*(After a quick look at GRANDMA, who nods)*
I do what I'm paid to do. I don't ask any questions.

MRS. BARKER

*(After a brief pause)*
Oh.
*(Pause)*
Well, you're quite right, of course, and I shouldn't meddle.

GRANDMA

*(To YOUNG MAN)*
Dear, will you take my things out to the van?
*(She points to the boxes)*

YOUNG MAN

*(After only the briefest hesitation)*
Why certainly.

GRANDMA

*(As the YOUNG MAN takes up half the boxes, exits by
the front door)*

Isn't that a nice young van man?

MRS. BARKER
*(Shaking her head in disbelief, watching the* YOUNG
MAN *exit)*
Unh-hunh . . . some things have changed for the better. I
remember when I had *my* mother carted off . . . the van man
who came for her wasn't anything near as nice as this one.

GRANDMA
Oh, did you have your mother carted off, too?

MRS. BARKER
*(Cheerfully)*
Why certainly! Didn't you?

GRANDMA
*(Puzzling)*
No . . . no, I didn't. At least, I can't remember. Listen dear; I
got to talk to you for a second.

MRS. BARKER
Why certainly, Grandma.

GRANDMA
Now, listen.

MRS. BARKER
Yes, Grandma. Yes.

GRANDMA
Now listen carefully. You got this dilemma here with
Mommy and Daddy . . .

MRS. BARKER

Yes! I wonder where they've gone to.

GRANDMA

They'll be back in. Now, LISTEN!

MRS. BARKER

Oh, I'm sorry.

GRANDMA

Now, you got this dilemma here with Mommy and Daddy,
and I think I got the way out for you.
*(The* YOUNG MAN *re-enters through the front door)*
Will you take the rest of my things out now, dear?
*(To* MRS. BARKER, *while the* YOUNG MAN *takes the
rest of the boxes, exits again by the front door)*
Fine. Now listen, dear.
*(She begins to whisper in* MRS. BARKER'S *ear)*

MRS. BARKER

Oh! Oh! Oh! I don't think I could . . . do you really think I
could? Well, why not? What a wonderful idea . . . what an
absolutely wonderful idea!

GRANDMA

Well, yes, I thought it was.

MRS. BARKER

And you so old!

GRANDMA

Heh, heh, heh.

MRS. BARKER

Well, I think it's absolutely marvelous, anyway. I'm going to find Mommy and Daddy right now.

GRANDMA

Good. You do that.

MRS. BARKER

Well, now. I think I will say good-by. I can't thank you enough.
*(She starts to exit through the archway)*

GRANDMA

You're welcome. Say it!

MRS. BARKER

Huh? What?

GRANDMA

Say good-by.

MRS. BARKER

Oh. Good-by.
*(She exits)*
Mommy! I say, Mommy! Daddy!

GRANDMA

Good-by.
*(By herself now, she looks about)*
Ah me.
*(Shakes her head)*
Ah me.

*(Takes in the room)*
Good-by.
*(The* YOUNG MAN *re-enters)*
Oh, hello, there.

YOUNG MAN

All the boxes are outside.

GRANDMA
*(A little sadly)*
I don't know why I bother to take them with me. They don't
have much in them . . . some old letters, a couple of regrets
. . . Pekinese . . . blind at that . . . the television . . . my
Sunday teeth . . . eighty-six years of living . . . some sounds
. . . a few images, a little garbled by now . . . and, well . . .
*(She shrugs)*
. . . you know . . . the things one accumulates.

YOUNG MAN
Can I get you . . . a cab, or something?

GRANDMA
Oh no, dear . . . thank you just the same. I'll take it from
here.

YOUNG MAN
And what shall I do now?

GRANDMA
Oh, you stay here, dear. It will all become clear to you. It will
be explained. You'll understand.

YOUNG MAN

Very well.

GRANDMA
*(After one more look about)*
Well . . .


YOUNG MAN
Let me see you to the elevator.


GRANDMA
Oh . . . that *would* be nice, dear.
*(They both exit by the front door, slowly)*
*(Enter* MRS. BARKER, *followed by* MOMMY *and*
DADDY)


MRS. BARKER
. . . and I'm happy to tell you that the whole thing's settled.
Just like that.


MOMMY
Oh, we're so glad. We were afraid there might be a problem,
what with delays, and all.


DADDY
Yes, we're very relieved.


MRS. BARKER
Well, now; that's what professional women are for.


MOMMY
Why . . . where's Grandma? Grandma's not here! Where's
Grandma? And look! The boxes are gone, too. Grandma's
gone, and so are the boxes. She's taken off and she's stolen
something! Daddy!

MRS. BARKER

Why, Mommy, the van man was here.


MOMMY

*(Startled)*

The what?


MRS. BARKER

The van man. The van man was here.

*(The lights might dim a little, suddenly)*


MOMMY

*(Shakes her head)*

No, that's impossible.


MRS. BARKER

Why, I saw him with my own two eyes.


MOMMY

*(Near tears)*

No, no, that's impossible. No. There's no such thing as the van man. There is no van man. We . . . we made him up. Grandma? Grandma?


DADDY

*(Moving to* MOMMY*)*

There, there, now.


MOMMY

Oh Daddy . . . where's Grandma?

DADDY

There, there, now.
(*While* DADDY *is comforting* MOMMY, GRANDMA
*comes out, stage right, near the footlights*)

GRANDMA
(*To the audience*)
Shhhhhh! I want to watch this.
(*She motions to* MRS. BARKER *who, with a secret
smile, tiptoes to the front door and opens it. The*
YOUNG MAN *is framed therein. Lights up full again
as he steps into the room*)

MRS. BARKER

Surprise! Surprise! Here we are!

MOMMY

What? What?

DADDY

Hm? What?

MOMMY
(*Her tears merely sniffles now*)
What surprise?

MRS. BARKER

Why, I told you. The surprise I told you about.

DADDY

You . . . you know, Mommy.

MOMMY

Sur . . . prise?


DADDY
(*Urging her to cheerfulness*)
You remember, Mommy; why we asked . . . uh . . . what's-
her-name-to come here?


MRS. BARKER

Mrs. Barker, if you don't mind.


DADDY

Yes. Mommy? You remember now? About the bumble . . .
about wanting satisfaction?


MOMMY
(*Her sorrow turning into delight*)
Yes. Why yes! Of course! Yes! Oh, how wonderful!


MRS. BARKER
(*To the* YOUNG MAN)
This is Mommy.


YOUNG MAN

How . . . how do you do?


MRS. BARKER
(*Stage whisper*)
Her name's Mommy.


YOUNG MAN

How . . . how do you do, Mommy?

MOMMY

Well! Hello there!

MRS. BARKER

*(To the* YOUNG MAN*)*
And that is Daddy.

YOUNG MAN

How do you do, sir?

DADDY

How do you do?

MOMMY

*(Herself again, circling the* YOUNG MAN, *feeling his arm, poking him)*
Yes, sir! Yes, sirree! Now this is more like it. Now this is a great deal more like it! Daddy! Come see. Come see if this isn't a great deal more like it.

DADDY

I . . . I can see from here, Mommy. It does look a great deal more like it.

MOMMY

Yes, sir. Yes sirree! Mrs. Barker, I don't know *how* to thank you.

MRS. BARKER

Oh, don't worry about that. I'll send you a bill in the mail.

MOMMY

What this really calls for is a celebration. It calls for a drink.

MRS. BARKER

Oh, what a nice idea.


MOMMY

There's some sauterne in the kitchen.


YOUNG MAN

I'll go.


MOMMY

Will you? Oh, how nice. The kitchen's through the archway there.
                    (As the YOUNG MAN exits: to MRS. BARKER)
He's very nice. Really top notch; much better than the other one.


MRS. BARKER

I'm glad you're pleased. And I'm glad everything's all straightened out.


MOMMY

Well, at least we know why we sent for you. We're glad that's cleared up. By the way, what's his name?


MRS. BARKER

Ha! Call him whatever you like. He's yours. Call him what you called the other one.


MOMMY

Daddy? What did we call the other one?


DADDY

        (Puzzles)
Why . . .

YOUNG MAN
*(Re-entering with a tray on which are a bottle of sauterne and five glasses)*
Here we are!

MOMMY
Hooray! Hooray!

MRS. BARKER
Oh, good!

MOMMY
*(Moving to the tray)*
So, let's— Five glasses? Why five? There are only four of us. Why five?

YOUNG MAN
*(Catches* GRANDMA'S *eye;* GRANDMA *indicates she is not there)*
Oh, I'm sorry.

MOMMY
You must learn to count. We're a wealthy family, and you must learn to count.

YOUNG MAN
I will.

MOMMY
Well, everybody take a glass.
*(They do)*
And we'll drink to celebrate. To satisfaction! Who says you can't get satisfaction these days!

MRS. BARKER

What dreadful sauterne!

MOMMY

Yes, isn't it?
*(To* YOUNG MAN, *her voice already a little fuzzy from the wine)*
You don't know how happy I am to see you! Yes sirree.
Listen, that time we had with . . . with the other one. I'll tell
you about it some time.
*(Indicates* MRS. BARKER*)*
I'll tell you all about it.
*(Sidles up to him a little)*
Maybe . . . maybe later tonight.

YOUNG MAN

*(Not moving away)*
Why yes. That would be very nice.

MOMMY

*(Puzzles)*
Something familiar about you . . . you know that? I can't
quite place it. . . .

GRANDMA

*(Interrupting . . . to audience)*
Well, I guess that just about wraps it up. I mean, for better or
worse, this is a comedy, and I don't think we'd better go any
further. No, definitely not. So, let's leave things as they are
right now . . . while everybody's happy . . . while everybody's
got what he wants . . . or everybody's got what he thinks he
wants. Good night, dears.

**CURTAIN**